DEMANDING HIS DESERT QUEEN

ANNIE WEST

MILLS & BOON

First Published in Great Britain 2019
by Mills & Boon, an imprint of HarperCollins*Publishers*
1 London Bridge Street, London, SE1 9GF

© 2019 Annie West

ISBN: 978-0-263-27101-0

MIX
Paper from
responsible sources
FSC C007454

This book is produced from independently certified FSC™ paper
to ensure responsible forest management.
For more information visit www.harpercollins.co.uk/green.

Printed and bound in Spain
by CPI, Barcelona

Growing up near the beach, **Annie West** spent lots of time observing tall, burnished lifeguards—early research! Now she spends her days fantasising about gorgeous men and their love-lives. Annie has been a reader all her life. She also loves travel, long walks, good company and great food. You can contact her at annie@annie-west.com or via PO Box 1041, Warners Bay, NSW 2282, Australia.

For Marianne Knip,
the first of my German readers I was lucky enough to meet.
Marianne, thank you for your continuing friendship.
Your warmth and your enthusiasm for my stories
are precious to me.
*Ich hoffe, wir begleiten weiterhin gemeinsam viele
Liebespaare auf ihren Weg ins Glück.*

CHAPTER ONE

'THE ANSWER IS NO.'

Karim's voice was harsher than usual, sharp rather than simply firm. The Assaran envoy's suggestion had stunned him. It seemed, despite his actions five years ago, he was still a part of Middle Eastern politics.

Karim stared through the window at the panorama of sapphire lake, verdant foothills and Swiss mountains, yet felt none of the calm the view was supposed to inspire. He spun around, ignoring the quickened beat of his pulse and the clench of his gut.

'But, Your Highness…'

Karim stiffened at the words. 'I no longer use a royal title.'

He watched the envoy absorb that.

'Sir, at least take time to consider. You haven't yet heard the Royal Council's reasoning.'

It was an enormous honour to be asked to take the Assaran throne. Especially since Karim wasn't Assaran. He came from the neighbouring kingdom of Za'daq, where his brother now ruled.

Karim wouldn't accept the Assaran crown. Yet he wondered why the Council was looking beyond its borders for a new sheikh. What about the heir? He knew the recently deceased ruler of Assara had left behind a wife and son.

When Karim realised the direction of his thoughts he

sliced them off. But not quickly enough to dispel the sour tang on his tongue.

'Please, sir.'

The man looked distressed. Karim knew his visitor would be blamed for failing in his mission. If it was discovered he'd been ejected by Karim in mere minutes...

Stifling a sigh, he gestured to the lounge. 'Take a seat. You might as well be comfortable.'

The presidential suite of this exclusive hotel might be comfortable, but sadly it hadn't proved exclusive enough to prevent this unwanted diplomatic delegation. As the hotel's new owner, Karim would change that.

'Thank you, sir.'

Even so, he waited till Karim had taken a seat facing him. Deference towards royalty was ingrained in the man. Even royals who'd renounced their regal claim.

For a mad moment Karim considered revealing the truth and ending this farce. But he'd vowed not to. His brother Ashraf had enough to deal with, imprinting his own stamp on Za'daq. He didn't need full-blown family scandal as well.

Their father had believed Ashraf, the younger brother, was the result of an affair between their mother and the man she'd later run off with. It had only been as the old Sheikh lay dying that they'd discovered Ashraf was legitimate.

Instead Karim, the firstborn, the one groomed from infancy to take the throne, was the cuckoo in the nest.

When, soon after, the old Sheikh had died, Karim had renounced the Za'daqi throne in favour of his brother. No one but the brothers knew the scandalous reason for his decision.

'The Council has given this its deepest consideration since the tragic death of our Sheikh.'

Karim nodded. The Assaran King's death had come out of the blue. 'But surely there's an heir?'

If the envoy noticed Karim's voice had turned to gravel, he didn't show it.

'Yes, but he's far too young to take up the reins of government. If the boy were older...a teenager, perhaps...a regent might be appointed to rule in his stead and help guide him. Given his extreme youth, the Council has decided unanimously that it's better for the country to find a new sheikh.'

'Thus disinheriting the child?' Karim had never met the boy. Intended never to meet him. Yet he felt for the child. His own brother would have been denied his true birthright if disapproving old men had had their way.

'Our constitution is different from yours in Za'daq, sir. In Assara what we propose is quite legitimate. The crown is passed from adult male to adult male.'

Karim nodded. This wasn't his battle to fight. He was only hearing the envoy out so the man could tell his masters he'd done his best.

'Surely there are suitable leaders in Assara? You don't need to go outside your country.'

Especially to a man who'd already turned his back on one sheikhdom.

The envoy pursed his lips, clearly taking time to choose his words. 'I need hardly say, sir, that the Council's deliberations are in strictest confidence.'

'Naturally.' Karim nodded. 'You have my assurance that nothing you say will leave this room.'

It would have been easier to end the meeting and send the man away. But Karim's curiosity was roused. He'd spent years building his investment business in lieu of ruling a country. But some things hadn't died—such as his interest in state affairs.

'Though the Sheikhs of Assara have been from the same family for over a hundred and fifty years, other significant families claim the right to offer a candidate in times where

the inheritance is...complicated. Several names have been put
forward. The one with the best claim is Hassan Shakroun.'

The visitor paused and Karim knew why. Shakroun was
a bully whose idea of negotiation was bluster and intimidation. He was interested in personal aggrandisement and
expanding his wealth, not in his nation. No wonder the Assarans were scoping other options for a king.

'I see you know the name.'

'We've met.' Once had been enough.

'Frankly, sir—' The man swallowed, then ploughed on.
'The Council is of the opinion that it's not bloodlines that
should determine our next leader so much as personal at-
tributes.'

Karim swallowed a wry smile. They certainly wouldn't
get royal bloodlines from him, even if his mother *was* from
a powerful family. His real father, as far as he could tell,
came from humble stock.

'You're after someone who will do the bidding of the
Council?'

It had been the same in Za'daq. Many councillors had
been close friends of the previous Sheikh and, influenced
by the old man's disdain for Ashraf, had made his suc-
cession difficult. Things were better now, but for a while
many had sought to bring Karim back and install him on
the throne. Which was one of the reasons he'd refused to
return to visit his homeland, except for Ashraf's wedding.
The other being that he knew it was better to cut all ties
rather than pine for what might have been.

'Not at all, sir.' The envoy interrupted his thoughts. 'The
Council wants a strong leader capable of taking responsibility. A man who knows diplomacy and statecraft. A
man who'll be respected by other rulers in the region. If
that man is from outside Assara, then it will short-circuit
internal squabbling between rival families with an interest in the throne.'

So he was to be the outsider who united the unsuccessful parties? The Assaran Council had a high opinion of his capabilities, if they believed him able to walk in, calm any fractious rivals and make a success of the role.

Once Karim would have been pleased at such proof of respect from a neighbouring government. He must have impressed them in his years helping his father rule Za'daq, trying to persuade the old man into modernisation.

But that had been then. This was now.

He couldn't accept the offer. Even if the Assarans did want him on merit rather than because of a royal pedigree. He'd built a new life. A life that hadn't been laid out for him because of his supposed lineage.

For thirty years he'd followed a narrow, straight path, putting work first, shouldering responsibility for others. He had been dutiful and decent, a hardworking, honourable prince.

Till his life had crumpled like tissue paper in an iron fist.

For a moment an image swam before him of wide brown eyes. Of a cupid's bow mouth. Of smashed hopes.

His breath hissed between his teeth as he banished the memory.

Karim was responsible for no one now but himself. That was exactly the way he wanted it. He knew the burden of being royal. He had no intention of putting on that yoke again.

'Please pass my compliments and thanks to your Royal Council. I'm deeply honoured that they should consider me for such a noble position.' He paused, watching his guest stiffen. 'However, my answer is still no.'

Safiyah stood in front of the mirror in her suite and tried to still the panic rising from her belly to her throat. She wiped her hands down her thighs, hating that they trembled.

It didn't matter what she wore. Yet she'd tried on every outfit she'd brought to Switzerland, finding fault with each one till all that had been left was this. A western-style dress, beautiful, in a heavy fabric that looked almost black. Until she moved. Then the light caught it and it glowed like deep crimson fire.

She bit her lip, suppressing a bitter laugh. Black and crimson. The colours of mourning and sacrifice. How apt. She'd done her share of both.

Safiyah shook her head, refusing to wallow in self-pity. She was far luckier than most. She had her health, a comfortable home and more money than she needed. Above all she had Tarek.

Life had taught her to set her shoulders and keep going, no matter what problems she encountered. To make the best of things and focus on others, not herself.

That was why she was here. To save someone precious. To save a whole nation if her fears were right.

She swung away, but stopped before the balcony and the spectacular view of lake and mountains. This was her first trip out of the Middle East and she felt like a country bumpkin, gawping at everything. Well, not everything. She knew about luxury, about limousines and discreet security guards. But those mountains! And the green that was so incredibly green! She'd seen photos, of course, but this was different. Even the air through the open window tasted unique, ripe with moisture and growing things.

In other circumstances she'd put on jeans and flat shoes and find a way to slip out of the hotel, away from the bodyguards. She'd stroll through the public gardens, take her time staring into the glittering shop windows, then go to the lake and sit there, soaking up the scenery.

But circumstances weren't different. Circumstances were difficult. Possibly dangerous, if the fears that kept her awake at night proved right and Hassan Shakroun took the throne.

Not surprising that her heart knocked against her ribs like a hammer on stone. Too much hung on this visit. Failure wasn't an option.

Safiyah's hand rose to her breastbone, her fingers touching the base of her throat as if to ease the riotous beat of her heart and the acid searing the back of her mouth.

It's fine to be nervous. That will keep you grounded so you don't get distracted by anything else.

Anything else being *him*—the man she'd travelled here to see. Even so, she'd hoped against hope it wouldn't be necessary. That things would be sorted without her involvement. She'd been appalled to learn nothing had been agreed. That she had to see him after all.

Just thinking of him made her insides clutch as if someone had wrapped a rope around her middle and yanked it mercilessly. Her blood pumped so fast it rushed in her ears.

That's good. The adrenalin will keep you alert. Give you courage.

Safiyah took a deep breath and smoothed her hands once more down her skirt. They were clammy, and her knees shook. But her dress covered her knees, and there'd be no handshake, so no one would know how nervous she was.

No matter what happened, she vowed one thing. She would not reveal weakness to this man.

Not after what he'd done to her before.

Ignoring the cold fingers dancing down her spine, Safiyah swung around and headed for the door.

'Her Highness, the Sheikha of Assara.'

The butler announced her in a slow, impressive tone that helped steady her jittering nerves.

This she could do. For years she'd compartmentalised, leaving the real her—Safiyah—behind and donning the persona expected of a queen, gracious and unruffled.

She lifted her chin, pinned on a calm expression that hid her inner turmoil and stepped into the suite's vast sitting room.

A few steps in and she paused, blinking against the light pouring in from the wall of windows. The butler bowed again and left, closing the door behind him with a quiet snick. It was only then that she made out a tall figure, motionless in the shadow just past the windows.

Even looking into the light, even unable to make out his features against the glare, she'd have known him. That rangy height, the sense of leashed energy. That indefinable shimmer in the air.

Her pulse quickened and her ribcage squeezed her labouring lungs. Fortunately she was old enough and experienced enough to know that this was her body's response to the pressure of her situation. It had nothing to do with feelings she'd once harboured.

'This is…unexpected, *Your Highness*.' His voice was whiplash-sharp as he used her title.

Good. She didn't want him trying his charm on her. Once bitten, twice shy. The thought steadied her nerves and stiffened her knees.

'Is it, Karim?'

Deliberately she used his first name. He might prefer to pretend they were strangers but she refused to rewrite the past to soothe his conscience. If he thought to intimidate, he'd discover she wouldn't yield meekly to a mere hint of displeasure. She'd had years to toughen up since they'd last met.

'I'd assumed, as the hotel owner, you'd be informed of royal guests.'

She stepped further into the room, onto a thick-pile carpet that would have taken a team of master weavers years to produce.

'Ah, but I'm here to conduct important business, not entertain passing acquaintances.'

As if she and her business were by definition unimportant. As if they had been mere acquaintances.

Safiyah had never been more grateful for those hard-learned lessons in self-control as his words ripped through to the small, vulnerable spot deep inside. To the tiny part of her that was still Safiyah, the eager innocent who'd once believed in destiny and happy endings.

Pain bloomed as if from a stabbing dagger. She breathed slowly and rode the hurt, forcing it down. 'My apologies for interrupting your…important business.' Pointedly she raised her eyebrows and glanced about the luxuriously furnished sitting room, as if expecting to see a conference table or a bevy of secretaries.

The voice inside told her not to rile him. She was supposed to persuade, even cajole him. But Safiyah refused to let him think he could brush her off.

'To what do I owe this…pleasure?'

There it was again, that emphasis that made it clear she was uninvited in his private space. Wounded pride made her want to lash out, but she reined in the impulse. She owed it to Tarek to stay calm.

'I need to talk with you.'

'About?'

Even now he didn't move closer. As if he preferred her to be at a disadvantage, unable to see him clearly while she stood in the full light from the windows.

She'd thought better of him.

'May I sit?' Did she imagine that tall body stiffened? She took her time moving to a cluster of chairs around a fireplace, then paused, waiting for an invitation.

'Please.'

Safiyah sank gracefully onto a seat and was glad of it, because when he moved into the light something inside her slipped undone.

Karim was the same, and yet more. The years had given his features a stark edge that accentuated his potent good looks. Once he'd been handsome. Now there was a gravity, an added depth that turned his slanted cheekbones, high-bridged nose and surprisingly sensual mouth into a face that arrested the breath in her lungs.

That black-as-night hair was shorter than before, close-cropped to his skull. That, too, reinforced the startling power of those masculine features. Then there were his eyes, dark moss-green, so intense she feared he saw beneath her façade of calm.

His clothes, dark trousers and a jacket, clearly made to measure, reinforced his aura of command. The snowy shirt emphasised the gold tone of his skin and she had to force herself not to stare at the space where the open top couple of buttons revealed a sliver of flesh.

Her breath snagged and a trickle of something she hadn't felt in years unfurled inside. Heat seared her cheeks. She didn't want to feel it. Would give anything *not* to feel it.

For a frantic moment Safiyah thought of surging to her feet and leaving. Anything rather than face the discomfiting stir of response deep in her feminine core.

This couldn't be happening! For so long she'd told herself her reaction to him all those years ago had been the product of girlish fantasy.

'My condolences on your recent loss.'

Karim's words leached the fiery blush from her face and doused the insidious sizzle of awareness. Shame enveloped her, leaving her hollow and surprisingly weak.

How could she respond like that to the mere sight of Karim when she'd buried her husband just weeks ago?

Abbas might not have been perfect. He might have been cold and demanding. But she owed his memory respect. He'd been her *husband*.

Safiyah looked at her clenched hands, white-knuckled in her lap. Slowly she unknotted them, spreading stiff fingers and composing them in a practised attitude of ease.

She lifted her head to find Karim sitting opposite her, long legs stretched out in a relaxed attitude. Yet his eyes told another story. Their gaze was sharp as a bird of prey's.

'Thank you.'

She said no more. None of the platitudes she'd hidden behind for the past few weeks would protect her from the guilt she harboured within. A guilt she feared Karim, with his unnerving perceptiveness, might somehow guess. Guilt because after the first shock of discovering she was a widow, and learning that Abbas hadn't suffered, she'd felt relief.

Not because she'd wanted her husband dead. Instead it was the relief of a wild animal held in captivity and suddenly given a glimpse of freedom. No matter how hard she tried, she hadn't yet managed to quell that undercurrent of excitement at the idea of taking control of her own life—hers and Tarek's. Of being simply…happy.

But it was too early to dream of freedom. Time enough to do that when she knew Tarek was safe.

'I'm waiting to hear the reason for your visit.'

Safiyah had imagined herself capable of handling most things life threw at her. She was stunned to discover Karim's brusque tone had the power to hurt.

She blinked, reminding herself that to hurt she would have to care about him, and she'd stopped caring long ago. She'd meant nothing to him. All the time he'd pretended to be interested in her he'd had other plans. Plans she hadn't understood and which hadn't included her. At best she'd been a smokescreen, at worst an amusement.

Safiyah lifted her chin and looked him full in the face, determined to get this over as soon as possible.

'I want you to take the Assaran crown.'

CHAPTER TWO

'YOU *WANT* ME to become your Sheikh?'

Karim's brow knitted. Before today he'd have said not much had the power to surprise him.

How wrong he'd been.

He'd assumed only self-interest would have budged Safiyah from the Assaran royal palace at such a time. He'd imagined she'd come here to dissuade him from accepting the sheikhdom.

Surely having him as her King would be the last thing she'd want? Shouldn't she be looking for ways to preserve the crown for her son?

'Yes. That's exactly what I want.'

Karim stared at the poised, beautiful woman before him. The whole day had been surreal, but seeing Safiyah again was the most extraordinary part of it.

The moment she'd walked into the room Karim's blood had thickened, his pulse growing ponderous. As if his body, even his brain, worked in slow motion.

He wasn't surprised that the shy young woman he'd known had disappeared. He'd long since realised her doe-eyed glances and quiet ardour had been ploys to snare his interest. The real Safiyah had been more calculating and pragmatic than he'd given her credit for.

Yet the change in her was remarkable. The way she'd sashayed into the room as if she owned it. The way she'd all but demanded he play by the rules and offer her a seat, as if they were polite strangers, or perhaps old friends about to enjoy a cosy chat.

But then life as an honoured and adored queen would give any woman confidence.

To Karim's chagrin, it wasn't merely her manner that got under his skin. Had her hourglass figure been that stunning when he'd known her? In the old days she'd worn muted colours and loosely fitting clothes, presumably to assure him that she was the 'nice' girl his father had assured him she was. The complete antithesis to the sultry sirens his brother had so scandalously bedded.

Safiyah's dress today might cover her from neck to shin, but the gleam of the fabric encasing those generous curves and tiny waist made it utterly provocative. Even the soft, sibilant *shush* of sound it made when she crossed her legs was suggestive.

Then there was her face. Arresting rather than beautiful. Pure skin, far paler than his. Eyes that looked too big as she stared back at him, as if hanging on his every word. Dark, sleek hair with the tiniest, intriguing hint of auburn. Lips that he'd once—

'Why do you want me to take the throne? Why not fight for your son's right to it?'

'Tarek is too young. Even if the Council could be persuaded to appoint a regent for him, I can't imagine many men would willingly take the role of ruler and then meekly hand it over after fifteen years.'

A man of honour would.

Karim didn't bother voicing the thought.

'Why not leave the decision to the Royal Council? Why interfere? Are you so eager to choose your next husband?'

Safiyah's breath hissed between pearly teeth and her creamy skin turned parchment-pale.

Satisfaction stirred as he saw his jibe hit the mark. For

he hated how she made him feel. She dredged up emotions he'd told himself were dead and buried. He felt them scrape up his gullet, across his skin. The searing hurt and disbelief, the sense of worthlessness and shock as his life had been turned inside out in one short night. At that crisis in his life her faithlessness had burned like acid—the final insult to a man who'd lost everything.

Nevertheless, as Karim watched the convulsive movement of her throat and the sudden appearance of a dimple in her cheek, his satisfaction bled away. Years ago she'd had a habit of biting her cheek when nervous. But Karim doubted nerves had anything to do with Safiyah's response now. Maybe she was trying to garner sympathy.

Yet he felt ashamed. He'd never been so petty as to take satisfaction in another's distress, even if it was feigned. He was better than that.

He opened his mouth to speak, but she beat him to it.

'I'm *not*...' she paused after the word, her chin tilting up as she caught his eye '...looking for a new husband.'

Her voice was low, the words barely above a whisper, yet he heard steel behind them.

Because she'd loved Abbas so deeply?

Karim found himself torn between hoping it was true and wanting to protest that she'd never loved her husband. Because just months before her marriage to the Assaran King she'd supposedly loved Karim.

He gritted his teeth, discomfited by the way feelings undermined his thought processes. He'd been taught to think clearly, to disengage his emotions, not to feel too much. His response to Safiyah's presence was out of character for a man renowned for his even temper, his consideration of others and careful thinking.

'That's not how things are done in Assara,' she added. 'The new Sheikh will be named by the Royal Council.

There is no requirement for him to marry his predecessor's widow.'

Was it his imagination, or had she shivered at the idea? She couldn't have made her disdain more obvious.

Which was tantamount to a lance, piercing Karim's pride. Once she'd welcomed his attentions. But then he'd been first in line to a royal throne of his own. The eldest son of a family proud of its noble lineage.

'What will happen to you when the new Sheikh is crowned?'

'To me?' Her eyes widened, as if she was surprised he'd even ask. 'Tarek and I will leave the palace and live elsewhere.'

Tarek. Her son.

He'd imagined once that she'd give him a son…

Karim slammed a barrier down on such sentimental thoughts. He didn't know what was wrong with him today. It was as if the feelings he'd put away years before hadn't gone away at all, but had festered, waiting to surge up and slap him down when he least expected it.

Deliberately he did what he did best—focused on the problem at hand, ready to find a solution.

'So if you have no personal interest in the next Sheikh, why come all the way here to see me? The Assaran envoy saw me a couple of hours ago. Couldn't you trust him to do the job he was chosen for?'

Karim knew something of Assaran politics. He couldn't believe the previous Sheikh had allowed his wife to play any significant role in matters of state. Whichever way he examined it, Safiyah's behaviour was odd.

'I didn't want to get involved.' Again her voice was low. 'But I felt duty-bound to come, just in case…' She shook her head and looked at a point near his ear. 'The Council is very eager to convince you. It was agreed that I should add my arguments if necessary.'

'And what arguments might those be?'

Karim kept his eyes fixed on her face. He wasn't tacky enough to stare at all the female bounty encased in rustling silk. But perhaps she'd guessed that he was wondering what persuasions she'd try. Colour streaked her cheekbones and her breasts lifted high on a suddenly indrawn breath.

'Assara needs you—'

'In case you haven't noticed, I'm not into a life of public service any more. I work for myself now.'

Her mouth settled in a line that spoke of determination. Had he ever seen her look like that? His memory of Safiyah at twenty-two was that she'd been gentle and eager to go along with whatever he suggested.

But that had been almost five years ago. He couldn't be expected to remember everything about her clearly, even if it felt like he did.

'I could talk about the wealth and honour that will be yours if you take the throne…'

She paused, but he didn't respond. Karim had his own money. He also knew that being Sheikh meant a lifetime of duty and responsibility. Riches and the glamour of a royal title didn't sway him.

Safiyah inclined her head, as if his non-response confirmed what she'd expected. 'Most important of all, you'd make a fine leader. You have the qualities Assara needs. You're honest, fair and hardworking. The political elite respect you. Plus you're interested in the wellbeing of the people. Everyone says it was you who began to make Za'daq better for those who weren't born rich.'

Karim felt his eyebrows climb. He was tempted to think she was trying to flatter him into accepting the position. Except there was nothing toadying about her demeanour.

'The nobles trust you. The people trust you.'

He shook his head. 'That was a long time ago.'

'Your qualities and experience will stand you in good

stead no matter how long it's been. And it's only been a few years.'

Years since he'd left his homeland and turned his back on everything he'd known. He was only now beginning to feel that he'd settled into his new life.

Safiyah leaned forward, and he felt for the first time since she'd arrived that she wasn't conscious of her body language. Earlier she'd seemed very self-aware. Now she was too caught up in their discussion to be guarded. He read animation in her brown eyes and knew, whatever her real reason for being here, that she meant what she said.

Karim canted closer, drawn to her in spite of himself.

'It's what you were born to do and you'd excel at it.'

Abruptly Karim sank back in his seat. Her words had unravelled the spell she'd woven. The moment of connection broke, shattered by a wave of revulsion.

'It doesn't matter what I was *born* to do.' His nostrils flared as he swallowed rising acid. 'I've renounced all that.'

Because he wasn't the man the world thought him. He was the bastard son of an unfaithful queen and her shadowy lover.

'Of course it matters!' Her clasped hands trembled as if with the force of her emotion. 'Assara desperately needs a ruler who can keep the country together—especially now, when rival clans are stirring dissension and jealousy. Each wants their own man on the throne.'

Karim shrugged. 'Why should I bother? One of them will be elected and the others will have to put up with it. Maybe there'll be unrest for a bit, but it will die down.'

'You don't see…'

She paused and looked down at her hands. Karim saw a tiny cleft appear in her cheek and then vanish. She was biting the inside of her mouth again. Absurdly, the sight moved him.

'What aren't you saying, Safiyah?'

It was the first time he'd spoken her name aloud in years. Her chin jerked up and for a moment her gaze clung to his. But he wasn't foolish enough to be beguiled by that haunted look.

See? Already it was gone, replaced by a smooth, composed mask.

'You're the best man for the role, Karim—far better than any of the other contenders. You'd make a real difference in Assara. The country needs a strong, honest leader who'll work for *all* his people.'

Karim digested that. Was she implying that her dead husband hadn't been a good ruler? The idea intrigued him. Or was she just referring to unrest now?

To his annoyance her expression gave little away. The Safiyah he'd once known, or thought he'd known, had been far easier to read. Even more annoying was the fact his interest was aroused by the idea of doing something intrinsically worthwhile. Something more meaningful than merely building his own wealth.

Karim frowned. How had Safiyah guessed such an appeal would tempt him?

He enjoyed the challenge of expanding his business interests. The cut and thrust of negotiation, of locating opportunities ripe for development and capitalising on them. That took skill, dedication and a fine sense of timing. Yet was it as satisfying as the work he'd been trained to do— using his skills to rule a nation?

The thought of Safiyah knowing him so well—better, it seemed, than he knew himself—infuriated him. This was the woman who'd spurned him when she discovered the secret taint of his illegitimacy. He'd believed in her, yet she'd turned her back on him without even the pretence of regret, much less a farewell. It galled him that anything she said could make him doubt even for a second his chosen course.

What was wrong with concentrating on his own life, his

own needs? Let others devote themselves to public service. He'd done his bit. Assara wasn't even his country.

Karim leaned back in his seat, raising his eyebrows. 'But I'm not a contender. I have already made that clear.'

He almost stood then, signifying the interview was over. But something prevented him. Something not at all fine or statesmanlike. An impulse grounded in the hurt he'd felt when she'd abandoned him.

'Unless…'

Satisfaction rose as she leaned closer, avid to hear more, her lush, cherry-red lips parted.

Karim had a sudden disconcerting memory of those lips pressed against his. They'd been devoid of lipstick and petal-soft. Her ardent, slightly clumsy kiss had enchanted and worried him. For, much as he'd wanted her, he had known he shouldn't seduce an innocent, even if they were on the verge of marriage. Especially an innocent who, with her father, was a guest in the royal palace.

Safiyah had been all the things Karim hadn't even known he wanted in a wife: generous, bright, shyly engaging and incredibly sexy. She'd been the reason he'd finally decided to give in to his father's demand that he marry.

'Unless?' Her voice was like honey.

'Unless there was more to the deal…an inducement.'

He leaned forward, and for a moment the space between them was negligible. He was close enough to see the tiny amber flecks in her brown eyes, to reacquaint himself with the creamy perfection of her skin and inhale a teasing drift of scent. A delicate floral perfume, with a warm, enticing undertone, that was unique to Safiyah.

That hint of fragrance hit him like a body-blow, sweeping him back to a time when he'd had everything. He'd been a prince, secure in his position, his place in the world and his family. He'd enjoyed his work, helping his father run Za'daq. He hadn't even regretted giving up his sexual freedom because Safiyah had turned the prospect of marriage from a duty to a pleasure.

'What sort of inducement?' Her voice was steady but her eyes were wary.

Karim told himself to leave it. To walk away. He had no intention of taking this further.

Then he heard his own voice saying, 'Marriage.'

He couldn't mean it.

He wasn't talking about marriage to *her*. Yet a strange shivery feeling rippled down her spine and curled into her belly like large fingers digging deep. Her skin prickled all over and heat eddied in disturbing places.

'I'm sure that will be no problem.' She forced a smile. 'You'll have your pick of eligible women.'

And Karim didn't need a crown or wealth to attract them. He was handsome, urbane and, she knew to her cost, charming. He could coax the birds from the trees if he set his mind to it. No wonder she, so unworldly and inexperienced at twenty-two, had been taken in, thinking his attentions meant something special.

'I don't need to pick when there's one obvious choice.'

His crystalline gaze locked on hers and his voice deepened to a baritone note she felt vibrate through her bones.

'The Queen of Assara.'

His words were clear. Safiyah heard them, and yet she told herself Karim had said something else. He couldn't really mean—

'*You*, Safiyah.'

'Me?' Her voice rose to a wobbly high note.

Once she'd believed he wanted to marry her, that he cared for her. Her father had been sure too. And so had Karim's father. He'd permitted her and her father to stay at the Za'daqi palace even while, as they'd discovered later, he was in the final stages of terminal illness.

But when a family emergency had dragged her and her father back to Assara everything had fallen apart. Karim hadn't farewelled them. Nor had he responded to the note she'd left him. A note she'd written and rewritten. There'd been no attempt to contact her since. Just...nothing. Not a single word. When she'd tried to contact him at the palace she'd been fobbed off.

Then had come the news that Karim's father had died. To everyone's amazement Karim had renounced the throne and left Za'daq. Even then she'd waited, refusing to believe he'd really abandoned her. Days had turned into weeks. Weeks to months. And still no word. And over those months her faith in him had shrivelled and turned into hurt, disbelief and finally anger.

Even at the last moment, when she'd been cornered in a situation she'd never wanted, a small, irrepressible part of her had hoped he'd step in and stop—

'Safiyah?'

She blinked and looked into that dark gaze. Once those eyes had glowed warm and she'd read affection there. Now they gave nothing away. The coldness emanating from him chilled her to the core.

'You want to marry *me*?' Finally she managed to control her vocal cords. The words emerged husky but even.

'Want...?' Forehead crinkling, he tilted his head as if musing on the idea. But the eyes pinioning hers held nothing like desire or pleasure. His expression was calculating.

That was what gave Safiyah the strength to sit up, spine stiff, eyebrows raised, as if his answer was only of mild interest. As if his patent lack of interest in her as a potential wife, a woman and a lover, didn't hurt.

She would *not* let him guess the terrible pain his indifference stirred. Everything inside her shrivelled. Bizarre that, even after his rejection years before, part of her had obstinately clung to the idea that he'd cared.

'You're right. No sensible man would *want* to marry a woman who ran out on him like a thief in the night.'

She gaped at the way he'd twisted the past. How dared he? Hearing the devastating news of her sister's attempted suicide, of *course* Safiyah and her father had gone to her immediately. Her father had made their apologies for the sudden departure, referring to a family emergency. Safiyah had assumed she'd have a chance to explain to Karim personally later.

Except he'd refused to take her calls. He'd led her on to believe he cared, then dumped her, and now he was pretending she'd been the one at fault!

'Now, look here! I—'

'Not that it matters now. The past is dead, not worth discussing.' He sliced the air with a decisive chopping motion, his expression cold. 'As for wanting marriage now... Perhaps *need* is a better word.' He opened those wide shoulders and spread his hands in a fatalistic gesture.

'I can't see your logic.'

Safiyah's voice was clipped, that of a woman ostensibly in control. She wouldn't demean herself by rehashing the past. He was right. It was over. She should count herself lucky she'd discovered Karim's true nature when she had. He hadn't been the paragon she'd believed.

'There's no reason for us to marry.'

'You don't think so?' He shook his head. 'I disagree. Despite what your law says, even the most optimistic supporter couldn't expect me to take the throne of Assara without a ripple. I'm a foreigner, an unknown quantity. You've said yourself that there are political undercurrents and rivalry in the country's ruling elite. To overcome those an incoming ruler would need to show a strong link to Assara and to the throne.'

He paused, watching her reaction. Now, with a sinking heart, Safiyah understood where he was going. And it made a horrible sort of sense.

'What better way of showing my respect for Assara and cultivating a sense of continuity than to marry the current Queen?'

Except said Queen would do just about anything to avoid another marriage. Particularly marriage to *this* man. Call it pride, call it self-preservation, but she'd be mad to agree.

'I disagree. With the Council's backing a newcomer, especially one with your qualities and experience, would be able to establish himself.' He was far, far better than the other alternatives.

Karim steepled his fingertips beneath his chin as if considering. But his response came so quickly she knew he'd immediately discounted her words.

'Besides, if I married you…'

Was it her imagination or did his voice slow on the words?

'Your son wouldn't be disinherited. That would satisfy any elements concerned at him being replaced by a foreigner. It would ensure the long-term continuity of the current dynasty.'

Safiyah sat in stunned silence, thinking through the implications of his words. 'You mean Tarek would be your heir? You'd adopt him?' The idea stunned her.

Emotion flickered across Karim's unreadable expression. 'I'm not a man who'd happily rip away someone's birthright, no matter what the constitution allows.'

There was something in his tone of voice, a peculiar resonance, that piqued her curiosity. Safiyah sensed there was more to his words than there seemed. But what?

She was on the verge of probing, till she read his body language. His hard-set jaw and flared nostrils revealed a man holding in strong emotion. Now wasn't the time to pursue this—not if she wanted him to take the throne.

Which was why she didn't instantly refuse. She needed time to persuade him.

'Are you saying if I agree to marry you...' she paused, fighting to keep her voice even '...you'd take the crown?'

His gaze sharpened. She felt it like an abrasive scrape across her flesh. The grooves bracketing those firm lips deepened, as if hinting at a smile, yet there was no softening in that austere, powerful face.

'I'm saying that if you agree to marry me I'll *consider* changing my mind about accepting the sheikhdom.'

Well, that put her in her place. Safiyah felt the air whoosh from her lungs, her chest crumpling with the force of that outward breath. Even if she agreed to marriage, it might not be enough to persuade him.

She'd never thought herself a particularly proud woman, but she hated that Karim had the power, still, to deflate her. To make her feel she was of no consequence. That incensed her.

For years she'd fought to maintain her self-respect and sense of worth, married to a man who adhered to the traditional view that a wife was merely an extension of her husband's will. Particularly a wife who'd been exalted by marrying a royal sheikh.

Fury surged at Karim's off-hand attitude. How dared he on the one hand ask her to marry him and on the other make it clear that even such a sacrifice on her part might not be enough to sway him?

Not that he'd *asked* her to marry him. He'd put it out there like some clause in a business contract.

Safiyah felt hot blood creep up her throat and into her cheeks. She wanted to let rip. To tell him he was an arrogant jerk, despite his royal blood. Her marriage had taught her that royals were no more perfect than anyone else. If anything, their ability to command not only great wealth, but the obedience of everyone around them, could amplify their character flaws.

But she didn't have the luxury of plain speaking. This wasn't about her. It was about Tarek's future, his safety. As well as the future of their country.

'What do you say, Safiyah? Is your country's wellbeing enough to tempt you into marriage again?' He sat back, relaxed in his chair, as if he didn't care one way or the other.

'There's something else.'

She'd hoped to persuade Karim without telling him of her fears, knowing he might well dismiss them since she had no proof. But what proof could she have till it was too late? The idea curdled her stomach.

'Another important reason for you to accept the throne. Hassan Shakroun—'

Karim cut her off. 'No more! I've already heard everything I need from the official envoy.'

As if *she*, the Queen of Assara, had no insight to offer! Perhaps he believed as Abbas had—that women weren't suited for politics. Or perhaps he was simply impatient that she hadn't leapt at the chance to marry him.

Safiyah was convinced Tarek would be in danger if Shakroun took the throne. She'd never liked the man, but the things she'd learned recently made her blood freeze at the idea of him in the palace. He wouldn't leave a potential rival sheikh with royal blood alive, even if that rival was a mere toddler.

Her throat closed, making her voice husky. 'But you must listen—'

'No.'

Karim didn't raise his voice, but that decisive tone stopped her.

'No more arguments. I don't *have* to listen to anything. You came to me, not the other way around.'

His words stilled her instinctive protest.

'I'm not inclined to accept the throne, but I'll consider it more thoroughly *if* you're willing to marry.'

Safiyah drew a deep breath, frantically searching for a semblance of calm. She couldn't believe the direction this conversation had taken. What had begun simply had become a nightmare.

She was about to ignore his warning and spill out her fears, but the stern lines of his expression stopped her. Karim didn't look like Abbas, but she recognised the pugnacious attitude of a man who'd made up his mind. Not just any man, but one raised to expect unquestioning obedience.

She'd learned with her husband that defiance of his pronouncements, even in the most trivial, unintended way, only made him less likely to listen. Safiyah couldn't afford to have Karim reject the crown.

Carefully she chose her words. 'I need time to consider too.'

Karim raised one supercilious eyebrow, obviously questioning the fact that she hadn't instantly leapt at the chance to marry him.

Except the thought of being tied in marriage to any man, especially Karim, sent a flurry of nervous dread through her.

'*You* need time?'

His tone made it clear he thought it inexplicable. He was right. Any other woman, she was sure, would jump at the chance to marry him.

'It seems we both do.' She held his gaze, refusing to look away. She might be reeling with shock inside, but she refused to betray the fact.

'Very well. We'll meet tomorrow at nine. A lot rides on your answer, Safiyah.'

CHAPTER THREE

'I LIKE IT,' Ashraf said over the phone. 'Accepting the Assaran crown is a perfect solution.'

Karim frowned at his brother's words as he wiped the sweat from his torso. The morning's visits had left him unsettled, and he'd sought to find calm through a workout in the gym, only to be interrupted by Ashraf's call.

'Solution? I don't see that there's a problem to be solved from your perspective—and especially not from mine.'

Yet, if not a problem, Karim sensed there was *something*. He and Ashraf had spoken at the weekend. It was unlike his brother to call again so soon. Unless something important had arisen. They didn't live in each other's pockets, but there was a genuine bond between them, all the more remarkable given the fact they'd been kept apart as much as possible by their father.

The old man had been prejudiced against Ashraf, believing him to be another man's son. He'd neglected the younger boy, fixing all his focus and energy on the elder. Not because he'd cared for Karim—the old tartar had been incapable of love—but because, as the eldest, he was the one to be moulded into a future sheikh.

If it hadn't been so personally painful Karim would have laughed when the truth had been revealed, that the Sheikh had picked the wrong heir. That Ashraf was the true son and Karim the bastard.

'I've no need of a throne, Ashraf. You know that.'

There was a growl in his voice. A morning besieged—first by the envoy from the Assaran Royal Council, and then by the only woman he'd ever seriously thought of marrying—had impaired his mood. The idea that Safiyah believed he still cared enough about her to be coaxed into doing her bidding set his teeth on edge. It would take more than an hour in the gym to ease the anger cramping his belly.

Karim stared through the huge windows, streaming with rain, towards the mountains, now shrouded in cloud. He usually found peace in a long ride. But he had no horses here. And even if he had, he wouldn't have subjected any poor beast to a hard ride in this weather just to shift his bad mood.

'Of course you don't need a throne.' Ashraf's tone was matter-of-fact. 'You've taken to being an independent businessman like a duck to water. Not to mention having the freedom to enjoy lovers without raising expectations that you're looking for a royal life partner.'

Karim's frown deepened. Did his brother miss his old life? Ashraf and Tori had been blissfully wrapped up in each other when he'd seen them last, but... 'What's wrong? Are you pining for your days as a carefree bachelor?'

Ashraf's laugh reassured him. 'Not a bit. I've never been happier.' He paused, his voice dropping to a more serious note. 'Except I'd rather you were here more often.'

It was a familiar argument, but Karim was adamant about not returning to Za'daq long-term. His brother was a fine leader, yet there were still a few powerful men who chafed at the idea of being ruled by a younger son.

His brother sighed at the other end of the line. 'Sorry. I promised myself I wouldn't mention it.'

'Why don't you just get to the point?'

The point being the outlandish suggestion that he,

Karim, should take the Assaran throne. Interestingly, the proposal hadn't been news to Ashraf. Nor did he think it outlandish.

'You rang to persuade me. Why?'

'Pure self-interest.' Ashraf's answer came instantly. 'Life will be much easier and better for our country if there's a stable government in Assara.'

Karim didn't dispute his logic. The two countries shared a border, and what affected one ended up affecting the other.

'If Shakroun becomes Sheikh there'll be stability.' Karim didn't like the man, but that was irrelevant. 'He's strong and he'll hang on to power.'

'That's what I'm afraid of,' his brother murmured.

'What?' Surely Ashraf wouldn't advocate civil unrest.

'You've been away a long time. Certain things have come to light that put a different slant on Shakroun and his activities.'

'I haven't heard anything.'

Despite removing himself from the Middle East, Karim followed press reports from the region. He'd told himself more than once that his interest in matters he'd left behind was a mistake, but though he'd cut so many ties he couldn't conquer his innate interest. He'd been bred to it, after all, had spent a lifetime living and breathing regional politics.

'We're not talking about anything known publicly. But a number of investigations are bearing fruit. Remember that people-smuggling ring that worked out of both countries?'

'How could I forget?'

Za'daq was a peaceable country, but years before the borderland between the two nations had been lawless, controlled by a ruthless criminal called Qadri. Qadri had unofficially run the region through violence and intimidation. One of his most profitable ventures had been people-smuggling from Za'daq into Assara and then to more distant markets. Tori, before she'd become Ashraf's wife, had been kidnapped for the trade, and Qadri had attempted to execute Ashraf himself.

'We don't have enough quite yet to prove it in a court of law, but we know Qadri's partner in the flesh trade was Hassan Shakroun.'

'I see...' The surprising thing was that Karim wasn't surprised. Not that he'd guessed Shakroun was a criminal. He'd just thought him deeply unpleasant and far too fixated on his own prestige and power. 'How sure are you?'

'I'm sure. The evidence is clear. But it will take time till the police are ready to press charges. Since Qadri's death Shakroun has taken over some of his criminal enterprises. They're trying to get an iron-clad case against him on a number of fronts. It's tough getting evidence, because Shakroun gets others to do his dirty work and witnesses are thin on the ground. A couple of people who stirred up trouble for him met with unfortunate "accidents".'

Karim felt an icy prickle across his rapidly cooling flesh. He grabbed a sweatshirt and pulled it one-handed over his head, then shoved his arms through the sleeves.

'That's one of the reasons the Council is searching for someone else to become Sheikh.'

Now it made so much more sense. Did Safiyah know?

Immediately he dragged his thoughts back. Safiyah wasn't the issue. He refused to be swayed by her. Yet the thought of her with her small child in the Assaran palace and Shakroun moving in made his stomach curdle.

'It's also why they're eager for an outsider,' Ashraf added. 'If they choose from within the country Shakroun is the obvious choice. He's from an influential family, and on the face of it would make a better leader than the other contenders. But with you they'd get someone they know and respect, who has a track record of ruling during those years when our father was ill.'

Karim let the words wash over him, ignoring Ashraf's reference to the man who'd raised him as his father. His thoughts were already moving on.

'How many know about this?'

'Very few. It's too early to accuse him publicly—not until the evidence is watertight. But if he becomes Sheikh...'

Karim could imagine. A criminal thug with almost absolute power. It didn't bear thinking about.

He ploughed his hand through his damp hair. 'It's still a matter for the Assarans.'

'And they want *you*, Karim.'

Karim's mouth flattened. His nostrils flared as he dragged in a deep breath. 'I've got a life here.'

He watched the stream of rain down the windows and another chill encompassed him. It didn't matter how long he spent in Europe and North America. He still missed the wide open skies of his homeland. The brilliant, harsh sun, and even the arid heartland where only the hardiest survived.

'I've got a business to run,' he added.

Ashraf didn't respond.

'I'm a private citizen now. I've had my fill of being royal. From the moment I could walk I was moulded into a prince, crammed full of lessons on public responsibility and politics. Now I'm living for myself.'

Not that he expected sympathy.

Finally his brother spoke. 'So you're telling me you'll just turn your back on the situation? Because you're having such a good time answering to no one but yourself?' He didn't hide his scepticism.

'Damn it, Ashraf! Do I look like a hero?'

His brother's voice held no laughter when he answered. 'I always thought so, bro.'

Karim flinched, feeling the twelve-month age difference

between them like a weight on his shoulders. Some hero! He hadn't been able to protect his own brother.

Karim had been a serious, responsible child, his world hemmed in by constant demands that he learn, achieve, excel, work harder and longer. Even so, he'd devoted himself to finding ingenious ways to keep the old Sheikh's attention off his younger brother. When he hadn't succeeded—when the old man had focused his hate on the boy he'd believed a bastard—Ashraf had been bullied and beaten. Karim hadn't been able to protect him all the time.

Ashraf had never blamed him for not looking after him better, but the twist of guilt in Karim's belly was something he'd always carry.

'You don't have to be a hero to become Sheikh,' Ashraf continued, as if he hadn't just shaken Karim to the core. 'Shakroun would have no qualms about taking the throne and there's nothing heroic about *him*. He'd enjoy the perks of the position.'

The words hauled Karim's thoughts out of the past and straight back to Assara. To the idea of Safiyah at the mercy of a man like Shakroun. Hassan Shakroun wouldn't be slow to recognise that tying himself to the previous Sheikh's beautiful widow would cement his position. Karim might not care for Safiyah any more but the thought of her with a thug like Shakroun...

Karim cursed under his breath, long and low. His brother, having made his point, merely said goodbye and left him with his thoughts.

Instinct warned Karim to keep a wide berth from Assara and its troubles. Yet his sense of responsibility nagged. It wasn't helped by the realisation, crystallised during the meeting with Safiyah, that his new life wasn't as fulfilling as he'd like. Yes, he had an aptitude for business and making money. Yes, he enjoyed the freedom to choose for himself, without pondering the impact of his decisions on millions of others. And Ashraf was right: it was far easier enjoying a discreet affair without the encumbrance of royalty.

But Karim had spent his life developing the skills to administer a nation. He'd had a few years of taking on more responsibility when the old Sheikh's health had faded. He'd thrived on it. It had been his vocation. Which was why he'd been so devastated when he'd had to step away. Ashraf had told him to stay as Sheikh but Karim hadn't been able to do it. His brother had already been robbed of so much. Karim had refused to take what was rightfully his.

The idea of making a real difference in Assara, doing what he was trained for and what he enjoyed, tempted him. He could do a lot for the place and its people. Assara was a fine country, but it was behind Za'daq in many ways. He'd enjoy the challenge.

Yet behind all those considerations was the thought of Safiyah. Of what would happen to her and her son if Shakroun became Sheikh.

Karim paced the private gym from end to end. Safiyah was nothing to him—no more important than any other Assaran citizen. He should be able to contemplate her without any stirring of emotion.

He grimaced. Emotion had lured him into playing out that scene with her earlier. He'd drawn out the interview with talk of marriage purely so he could watch her squirm. It had been a low act. Karim was ashamed of stooping to it. He couldn't recall ever deliberately lying before. But he'd lied blatantly today. To salve his pride. And because he hated the fact that Safiyah could make him feel anything when she felt nothing. To her he was, as he'd always been, a means to an end.

But his talk of marriage had backfired mightily.

Because now he couldn't get it out of his head.

Karim was intrigued by her. He kept circling back to the

idea of Safiyah as his lover. Maybe because although they'd once been on the verge of betrothal, they'd never shared more than a few kisses. The night she'd agreed to come to him had been the night his world had been blown apart.

That had to be the reason he felt so unsettled. Safiyah was unfinished business.

Lust speared him, dark and urgent, as he remembered her in the crimson dress that had clung like a lover's hands. The delicate pendant she'd worn, with a single glowing red stone, had drawn his eyes to the pale perfection of her throat. He'd wanted to bury his face where her pulse beat too fast and find out if she was still as sensitive there as he remembered. Or if that too had been a hoax. Like the way she'd pretended to fall for him.

He knew he should walk away.

Safiyah tested his limits more than any woman he'd met. He didn't want to spend his life with a woman he couldn't trust or respect. Even to satisfy his lust.

But what if he did walk away? If he let Shakroun take the throne?

Karim would be in part responsible for what that thug did to Assara. And what he might do to Safiyah and her boy.

Karim stopped pacing and stared at the tall figure reflected in the mirror on the far side of the room. He saw hands clenched into fists, tendons standing taut, a body tensed for action.

He'd been raised to put the welfare of a nation before his own. That conditioning was hard to break.

Surely *that* was what made him hesitate.

He had a major decision to make and it would *not* hinge on Safiyah.

Karim forked his hand through his hair, scraping his fingers along his scalp. The trouble was, the more he thought about it, the more he realised marriage to the Assaran Queen was the best way to ensure he was accepted as Sheikh.

If he chose to take the role.

If he could bring himself to marry the woman who'd once spurned him.

'He's *fine*, Safiyah. Truly. It was just a runny nose and he's okay now. He's bright as anything and he's been playing with the puppies.'

The phone to her ear, Safiyah rolled onto her back on the wide bed, imagining Tarek with a tumble of puppies. He'd be in his element. He loved animals, but Abbas had always said a palace was no place for pets.

'You brought them to the palace on purpose, didn't you, Rana? You're hoping we'll keep one.'

Not that she minded. These last few years she'd missed being around dogs and horses. There was something soothing about their unquestioning love.

'Guilty as charged.'

Her sister's chuckle made Safiyah smile. It was such a carefree sound, and one she still cherished. Rana was happy and settled now—such a tremendous change from a few years ago.

'But you know how hard it can be to find homes for a litter. Especially since they're not pure-bred. What's *one* little puppy…?'

Safiyah laughed at Rana's exaggerated tone of innocence. 'Probably a lot of trouble until it's house-trained and learns not to chew everything in sight. But you're right. A dog would be good company for Tarek.'

Not that her son showed any sign of missing Abbas. He'd rarely seen his father more than once a week, and then only for short periods, usually in the throne room or the royal study.

Those meetings had been formal affairs. Abbas hadn't

been one to cuddle his son, or play games. He'd said that was how royal heirs were raised. They weren't supposed to cling to their parents. And besides, as Sheikh he'd had other things to keep him busy. He'd assured Safiyah that when Tarek was old enough he'd take him in hand and teach him what he needed to know to rule Assara.

That was never going to happen now.

Tarek would grow up without knowing his father.

Nor would he become Sheikh.

A pang of fear pierced her chest. Would her son be allowed to grow up in safety? What would happen if Karim didn't take the crown? He'd looked anything but happy about the idea. But if he didn't and Hassan Shakroun became Sheikh—

'Safiyah? Are you still there?'

'Sorry, Rana. I got distracted.'

'Things didn't go well?'

'I'm sure it will work out just fine.' Safiyah was so used to putting a positive spin on things, protecting her sister as much as possible, that the words emerged automatically.

'Reading between the lines, it doesn't sound like it.' Rana paused, then, 'You *can* talk to me, you know, Safiyah. I'm not as fragile as I used to be.'

'I know that.'

These days Rana seemed a different person entirely from the severely depressed young woman she'd once been. It was habit rather than need that fed Safiyah's protectiveness, yet old ways died hard.

'But there's no news yet—nothing to share.'

Other than the fact Karim had asked her to be his wife.

No, not asked. Demanded. Made it a condition of him even considering accepting the sheikhdom.

She couldn't share that fact. Not till she'd worked out what answer she was going to give.

Marrying Karim seemed impossible. Especially as

there'd been not even a hint of warmth when he spoke of it. Instead he'd looked so cold, so brooding...

She *couldn't* say yes. The very thought of accepting another marriage of convenience when she'd just escaped one sent shivers scudding down her spine.

Naturally they were shivers of distaste. They couldn't be anything else.

But if she said no what would happen to Tarek? She'd do whatever it took to see him safe. Of course she would. Yet surely there was some other way. Surely marriage wasn't essential.

'Well, if you need to talk I'm just here.'

It struck Safiyah how far Rana had come from the troubled girl she'd been. 'Thank you, Rana. I'm so lucky to have you.' Especially as a few short years ago Safiyah had almost lost her. 'To be honest, I—'

A knock on the door interrupted her. 'Sorry, there's someone here. I'll just see who it is.'

Safiyah swung her bare feet off the bed, retying the belt of her long robe. She glanced at the time. Nine o'clock. Too late for a casual visitor, even if she'd known anyone else in Switzerland. And the special envoy who'd accompanied her from Assara would never dream of simply turning up at her door. He'd ring first.

'That's fine. I need to go anyway.'

In the background Safiyah heard yapping. She grinned as she crossed the bedroom and entered the suite's sitting room, flicking on a lamp as she went.

'Okay. Give Tarek a hug and kiss from me and tell him I'll be home soon.'

'I will. And good luck!'

More yapping, this time more frenzied, and Rana hung up.

Safiyah reached the entrance of her suite and peered through the peephole. Her vision was obscured by a large fist, raised to knock. When it lowered she was looking at a broad chest, straight shoulders and the dark gold flesh of a masculine neck and jaw.

Karim!

Safiyah's pulse catapulted against her ribs, taking up a rackety, uneven beat. They'd agreed to meet tomorrow morning. Not tonight. She wasn't prepared.

She glanced down at the silk robe of deep rose-pink. It covered her to her ankles, but abruptly Safiyah became aware that beneath it she wore nothing but an equally thin nightgown.

That hand rose to knock again, and she knew she had no choice but to answer.

She cracked the door open, keeping out of view behind it as much as possible.

'Karim. This is a surprise.' Despite her efforts her voice sounded husky, betraying her lack of calm.

'Safiyah.' He nodded and stepped forward, clearly expecting her to admit him.

She held the door firmly, not budging. 'It's late. I'm afraid it's not convenient to talk now.' Not when she was barefoot and wearing next to nothing. 'Can this wait till the morning?'

By then she'd have some idea of what she was going to say. Hopefully. Plus she'd be dressed. Definitely. Dressed in something that didn't make her feel appallingly feminine and vulnerable just standing close to Karim.

Was she entertaining a lover? The idea flashed into his brain, splintering thoughts of sheikhdoms and politics.

Her cheeks were pink and her hair was a messy dark cloud drifting over her shoulders, as if she'd just climbed out of bed. Her eyes shone like gems and he saw the pulse jitter at the base of her throat, drawing attention both to her elegant neck and her agitation.

Karim's pulse revved as he propped the door open with his shoulder. He heard no noise in the room behind her but that meant nothing.

'I'm afraid this can't wait.'

Wide eyes looked up at him. Still she didn't move. He watched her swallow, the movement convulsive. Karim felt a stab of hunger. He fought the urge to stroke that pale skin and discover if it was as soft as he remembered.

Such weakness only fired his annoyance. Bad enough that his every attempt to think logically about this situation and his future kept swinging back to thoughts of Safiyah. Karim chafed at his unwanted weakness for this woman.

'Surely tomorrow—'

'Not tomorrow. Now.' He bent his head, bringing it closer to hers. 'If I walk away now, Safiyah, don't expect me ever to walk into Assara.'

He didn't mention the sheikhdom. Even in this quiet corridor he was cautious with his words, but she understood. He saw the colour fade from her cheeks and she stepped back, allowing him to enter.

One quick, comprehensive survey revealed that she wore silk and lace. Her robe clung to an hourglass figure that would make any man stare. Especially when she swung round after shutting the door and her full breasts wobbled with the movement, clearly unrestrained by a bra. That wobble shot a dart of pure lust to his tightening groin.

Karim guessed her robe had been put on quickly. It was belted, but gaped open over a low décolletage, over creamy, fragrant flesh and more pink silk. Even the colour of the silk was flagrantly feminine.

A flicker of long-buried memory stirred...of his mother's private courtyard, filled with the heady scent of damask roses, their petals a deep, velvety pink. It had been an oasis of femininity in his father's austere palace. And it had been razed to bare earth when the old man had discovered her sons, at four and three respectively, were pining for her after she'd run off with her lover and had secretly sought solace in her garden.

But memories of the past faded as he took in Safiyah, looking lush and sensual. Outrageously inviting. Especially with that cloud of dark hair spilling around her shoulders, the ends curling around her breasts.

Had some lover been fondling those breasts? Was that why her hard nipples thrust against the silk?

Heat drenched Karim as he flexed his hands and made himself turn from temptation. He strode into the sitting room, giving it a cursory survey before following the light into her bedroom. The bed was still neatly made, but a pile of pillows was propped up on one side. She'd been sitting there alone.

The knowledge smacked him in the chest, stealing both his air and his sense of indignation.

'What are you doing?'

Her voice came from just behind him. It sounded husky, and something drew tight in his groin.

'Nice suite.' He turned and gave her a bland look. 'I hadn't seen it before.' With luck she'd think that as the hotel's new owner he was simply curious about the accommodation.

He walked back into the sitting room and heard the bedroom door snick shut behind him.

Wise woman.

'What is it that can't wait?'

Karim swung round to find her closer than he'd expected. She'd adjusted her robe so barely a sliver of flesh showed beneath the collarbone and she was busily knotting the belt cinching her waist. As if a layer of silk could conceal her seductive body.

'Things are moving quickly.'

That was one thing his deliberations and a second discussion with the Assaran envoy had made clear. If he was going to accept the crown he needed to act fast—before Shakroun got wind of the attempt to bring in an outsider. The man could stir all sorts of trouble.

'I need your answer now.'

'Oh.' She frowned. 'My answer.'

Safiyah looked distracted. As if her mind were elsewhere, rather than on the honour he'd done her by suggesting marriage so she could retain her royal status.

Karim gritted his teeth, fury rising. She acted as if his suggestion they marry was trivial. Not enough to hold her interest when she had more important things on her mind. And this after the insult of her desertion five years before. It was more than his pride could bear.

Something ground through him like desert boulders scraping together, the friction sparking an anger he'd harnessed for so long.

Karim had spent a lifetime being reasonable, honourable, and above all rational. He'd been trained never to act rashly. To weigh his options and consider the implications not only for himself but for others.

Not tonight.

Tonight another man inhabited his skin. A man driven by instincts he'd repressed for years.

'What is it, Safiyah?' He took two paces, stopping only when she had to hike her chin high to hold his eyes. 'You've got something else on your mind? Is it this?'

He cupped one hand around the back of her head, anchoring his fingers in that lush, silky hair.

No protest came. His other arm wrapped around her waist, tugging her close. He had a moment of heady anticipation as her soft form fell against him, her eyes growing huge and dark as pansies.

Then his mouth settled on hers and the years were stripped away.

CHAPTER FOUR

SAFIYAH CLUNG TIGHT, her fingers embedded in the hard biceps that held her to Karim's powerful frame. It was so unexpected she had no time to gather her thoughts. No time to do anything but bend before the force of sensations and emotions that made her sway like a sapling in a strong wind, her body arching back over his steely arm.

To her shame it wasn't outrage that overwhelmed her. It was shocked delight.

Because she'd never been kissed like this.

Never felt like this.

Not even in those heady days when Karim had courted her, for then he'd been considerate and careful not to push her into a compromising position. She'd been innocent and he'd respected that.

Even when she'd married she hadn't felt like this.

Especially when she'd married. She'd felt no passion for Abbas. No desire except the desire to do her duty. And Abbas, though he'd enjoyed her body, hadn't expected anything from her other than acquiescence.

Which made the fire licking her veins unprecedented. Totally new.

Safiyah shivered—not with cold, but with a roaring, instantaneous heat that ignited deep inside and showered through her like sparks from a bonfire, spreading incendiary trails to every part of her body.

This was passion.

This was desire.

It was like the yearning she'd once felt for Karim, multiplied a thousandfold. Like the difference between the heat of a match and the scorch of a lightning strike.

Her mouth opened, accommodating the plunging sweep of his tongue, relearning Karim's darkly addictive taste. It was a flavour she'd made herself forget when she'd told herself to stop pining for the mirage of true love. When she'd given herself in a dutiful arranged marriage.

Because to hold on to those broken dreams would only have destroyed her.

Now, with a force that shook her to the core, Safiyah felt them flood back, in a deluge of sensation to a body starved of affection, much less delight.

Once Safiyah had yearned for Karim with all her virgin heart. Now, time, experience and loss had transformed her once innocent desire into something fierce and elemental. Something utterly unstoppable.

Instead of submitting meekly, or turning away, Safiyah leaned into his hard frame. It felt as natural as smiling. As necessary as breathing.

Her tongue slid the length of his, exploring, tasting, enjoying the rich essence of sandalwood and virile male that filled her senses. She revelled in the feel of his taut frame solid against hers and rose onto her toes to press closer.

A shudder passed through him and his hands tightened possessively, as if her response unleashed something in him that he'd kept locked away. He leaned in, forcing her head back, deepening the kiss, and she went willingly, exulting in the breathtaking intensity of the moment.

Past and future were blotted out. The present consumed her. Her need for this, for him. Nothing else mattered except assuaging that.

Karim's arm slid down her back, his palm curving over

her backside, lifting her towards the drenching heat of his muscled frame. Excitement tore through her, a fierce exhilaration as she read the tension of a man on the brink of losing himself.

Then, with an abruptness that left her swaying, he released her.

Blinking, Safiyah watched him step back. Saw his mouth lengthen in a grimace. Saw him shrug those broad shoulders and straighten his jacket as if brushing off the imprint of her clawing hands. Then he shoved both fists in his pockets and lifted one eyebrow in an expression of cool enquiry.

Flustered, Safiyah felt her heart smash against her ribs, her breasts rising and falling too fast as she tried, unsuccessfully, to get her breathing back to normal.

Her robe had come undone and she knew without looking that her nipples were hard, needy points against the thin fabric of her nightdress. Worse, between her legs was a spill of dampness. Restlessness filled her, and the need to climb up that big body and rub herself against him, chasing the fulfilment that no-holds-barred kiss had promised.

Instead she stood stock-still, feet planted. Mechanically her hands grabbed the sides of her robe and tied it tight. Because, despite the thwarted desire churning through her, Safiyah read the chill in those green eyes surveying her like an insect on a pin. Her skin turned to gooseflesh and the fine hairs at her nape stood on end.

Karim wasn't even breathing heavily. He looked as calm and remote as a stone effigy. And as welcoming.

Looking into those austere features, Safiyah felt all that lush heat dissipate. Instead of his deliciousness she tasted the ashes of passion. She might have been swept away by forces she couldn't control but Karim hadn't.

'Well, that little experiment was instructive.' His voice came from a great distance, like low thunder rolling across the wide Assaran plain. 'It's as well to test these things in advance, isn't it?'

'Test what?' Her voice was husky, but reassuringly even. She'd had years of practice at perfecting a façade that hid her feelings.

Those powerful shoulders shrugged nonchalantly. 'Our physical compatibility.' He paused, his gaze capturing hers as he continued with conscious deliberation, 'Or lack of it.'

Deep, deep inside, in that place where she'd once locked her secret hopes and cravings, something crumpled and withered. There was an instant of shearing pain, like a knife-jab to the abdomen. Then it morphed into an unremitting ache that filled her from scalp to toe.

He'd kissed her like that as an *experiment*?

Safiyah wanted to scream and howl. To pummel that granite-hard chest with her fists. But that would achieve nothing except further embarrassment.

A new kind of fire bloomed within her and seared her cheeks. *Shame.* Shame that she'd responded to this man who now surveyed her with such detachment. Shame that she'd ever been attracted to him.

Swallowing the tangled knot of emotion clogging her throat was almost impossible. Finally she managed, though it physically hurt.

Pain was good, Safiyah assured herself. Pain would make it easier to strip away the final fragments of feeling she'd harboured for Karim.

She'd repressed her feelings for years, told herself she couldn't possibly still want this man who'd rejected her. Whose abandonment had devastated her and branded her with a bone-deep disdain for him and his callous ways.

Yet once in his arms, once his mouth had met hers, she'd responded with an ardour that had been nothing short of embarrassing.

Even now part of her protested. He *had* responded. He'd

wanted to follow that kiss to its natural conclusion just as she had.

Then her brain began to work. People pretended all the time. Hadn't she pretended enthusiasm for Abbas in her bed even when she'd far rather have slept alone? Just because Karim's kiss had been passionate, it didn't mean he'd felt anything but curiosity.

The inequality of their experience told against her. She'd only kissed two men in her life: Karim and her husband. And no kiss before today had awakened such a powerful response in her. Whereas Karim had had women following him, sighing over him and trying to capture his interest for years. No doubt he'd kissed hundreds of women and could feign sexual interest.

He wasn't interested now.

Safiyah's mouth firmed. '*If* I were to marry you...' her words dripped acid '...it wouldn't be for the pleasure of your company.'

Let him read what he liked into her response. She refused to admit anything. After all, she could claim that, like him, she'd been experimenting, searching but not finding a spark between them.

Except she'd never been a liar. The knowledge of her complete submission to Karim's demanding kiss devastated her. She wanted to turn tail and hide.

'Then why *would* you agree to marry me?'

It was a timely reminder, and it stiffened her wobbly knees. She met Karim's stare head-on. 'For my country and my son. I'm afraid of what might happen to both if Shakroun becomes Sheikh.'

Slowly he nodded. 'I understand. I've been hearing more about him this evening.'

Relief made her shoulders sag. Karim sounded like a man who'd changed his mind. If he took the throne Tarek would be safe.

'But what I've heard only reinforces what I said earlier. He's from a powerful clan. If I became Sheikh I'd need to do everything I could to shore up local support. Like marry you.'

Karim's deep voice and narrowed eyes held nothing soft. His needle-sharp scrutiny grazed her skin and her pride. Safiyah might have let him make a fool of her years ago, and again just now, but no more. Enough was enough.

'*If* I were to marry you...' How the thought appalled. But Safiyah would sacrifice her freedom ten times over for her son's life. 'I'd expect you to take your pleasure outside the marriage bed.' She almost choked on the word 'bed', but forced herself to carry on as if unfazed by that kiss. 'Discreetly, of course.'

'Would you, indeed?' Something dark flashed in Karim's eyes. 'And where would you...take *your* pleasure?'

Safiyah stood as tall as she could, lengthening her neck and calling on all the lessons in dignity she'd learned in the past few years. 'That needn't concern you. Rest assured I won't cause any scandals.'

Because sex with Abbas hadn't left her with a burning desire for more. And the one man who'd had the power to wake her libido was staring at her now as if she were something he'd picked up on the sole of his shoe.

Safiyah blocked the jumble of hurt and indignation writhing within, shoving it away with all the other hurts and disappointments she couldn't afford to think about. Instead she concentrated on playing the part of Queen, as her dead husband had taught her. And instead of her usual composure, she aimed for a touch of Abbas's condescension. Presumably it worked, for Karim's dark eyebrows climbed high.

'And if I want pleasure *within* the marriage bed?'

The silky words drew her up short, made her pulse accelerate wildly.

Karim wanted sex with her?

Or was he just trying to make her squirm?

Her hair brushed her cheeks as she shook her head. 'No.'

'Because you don't want me, Safiyah? Or because you're scared you want me too much?'

'Your ego is monumental, Karim.' Adrenaline shot through her and her jaw tilted imperiously.

He merely shrugged. 'I call it as I see it. From where I stand I suspect you're not as uninterested as you say. But I would never force myself on an unwilling woman.'

Safiyah exhaled slowly, trying to banish that panicky feeling. 'I have your word on that?'

'You do.' He paused to let her absorb the words. 'No sex unless you want it, Safiyah. Does that satisfy you?'

She surveyed him carefully. Surely this was just macho male posturing because she'd said she didn't want him. Karim would soon find some ravishing mistress to keep him occupied.

He might be the man who'd dumped her, but she believed him too proud to break his word. Clearly the Council thought the same. And when it boiled down to it what real choice did she have? She needed to save Tarek.

Finally she nodded. 'Yes.'

'You actually trust my word?' His cool tone and the jut of his jaw spoke of haughty male pride.

'Yes.'

Still his frown lingered.

'After all, I'd be entrusting you with my son's wellbeing.'

Saying it aloud sent a shiver rippling down her spine. Not because Karim would hurt them, but at the idea of tying herself once more to a man who saw her as a mere convenience. But she'd survived that once. She could again.

Safiyah returned his stare with one of her own, trying not to catalogue those spare, attractive features she'd once daydreamed about. She reminded herself that he was arrogant and unfeeling, a man who'd toyed with her.

What had happened to the man she'd fallen for at twenty-two? Had she been completely misled by his charm and apparent kindness? What had made him cold and bitter? The same mysterious thing that had driven him to give up his throne?

It didn't matter. She wasn't about to pry into his past or his character, beyond the fact that he would do the right thing. When it came to his honour, and his work for his people, Karim's record was strong. The Royal Council wouldn't have made its offer if there were doubts. It had deliberated carefully before approaching Karim, investigating not only his years in Za'daq but his recent activities.

Nevertheless…

'If you become Sheikh, what about my son, Tarek? Are you serious about adopting him?'

Karim inclined his head. 'I told you before—I'm not the man to steal your son's birthright. He'll still be in line to become Sheikh eventually.'

It seemed too good to be true. If anyone else had said it Safiyah would have doubted they meant it. But Karim had already walked away from one throne. It was still on the tip of her tongue to ask what had prompted that action, but she kept silent. That didn't matter now. As he'd said earlier, the past was best left alone. All that mattered was Tarek's safety and Assara's.

She clasped her hands at her waist and stood silent, watching him. He couldn't have made it clearer that he saw marriage to her as a necessity, not a pleasure. And she should be used to being viewed as a political expedient.

Yet still it hurt!

Abbas had married her because it had suited him to build an alliance with her clan, so when the time had come for him to marry he'd turned his eyes to her family. At first he'd been interested in her clever younger sister, studying at university in the capital. When that hadn't been possible he'd made do with Safiyah.

To accept a second marriage of convenience, to another man who had no feelings for her, was a terrible thing. So terrible Safiyah wanted to smash something. To tell Karim in scathing detail what he could do with his marriage plans.

But she loved her son too much. She'd do anything to keep him safe. Her happiness meant nothing against that. And as for the dreams she'd once harboured of finding love…

Safiyah shuddered and rubbed her hands up her arms. As a twenty-seven-year-old widow she'd be a fool to believe in romance.

'What are you thinking?'

Karim hadn't come closer, yet his voice curled around her. She stiffened and moved to the window, needing distance from his looming presence. She looked out at the sprinkle of lights in the darkness, where the town bled down the slope towards the lake.

'What if you have children? Wouldn't you want them to inherit? I can't believe you'd put your own flesh and blood second to someone else's.'

Safiyah spun around to find him watching her, his expression intense yet impenetrable. Before she could puzzle over it he spoke.

'Don't worry, Safiyah, I won't foist any bastard children on you.'

His tone cut like a blade and his brow wrinkled into a scowl, making her wonder at the depth of his anger. For anger there was, vibrating through the thickening atmosphere.

Safiyah tried to fathom it. Even when she'd told him he could forget about sharing her bed she hadn't sensed fury like this.

Then, as abruptly as it had surfaced, it disappeared.

'So, you agree to marry me?'

He still didn't approach. Didn't attempt to woo her with soft words or tender caresses.

Safiyah told herself she was grateful.

'I...' The words stuck in her throat. Duty, maternal love, patriotism—all demanded she say yes. Yet it was a struggle to conquer the selfish part of her that wanted something for herself. Finally she nodded. 'Yes. If you take the throne, I'll marry you.'

She hadn't expected a display of strong emotion, but she'd expected *something* to show he appreciated her sacrifice. Even a flicker in that stern expression.

She got nothing.

'Good. We'll travel to Assara tomorrow.'

Karim kept his tone brisk, masking the momentary flash of emotion that struck out of nowhere and lodged like a nail between his ribs.

He inhaled, drawing on a lifetime's training in dismissing inconvenient feelings. He didn't *do* sentiment.

'Tomorrow?'

Her eyes rounded. Almost as if she didn't want this. Didn't want *him*.

'I'll accept the Council's offer in person. Now I've decided there's no time to be lost. There's no point giving Shakroun any opportunity to build more support.'

It would be a long, tough road ahead, establishing himself as Sheikh in a foreign country. Karim was under no illusions about that. But excitement burgeoned at the prospect. It was the work he'd been bred to, the work he'd missed even if he hadn't allowed himself to admit it.

And nor was it just the work he looked forward to.

He watched Safiyah watching him and kept his face studiously blank. It wouldn't do to let her guess that one of the benefits in acting quickly was to secure her.

Purely for political reasons, of course.

Yet Safiyah unsettled him more than she should. Thoughts of her had interfered with his decision-making and he'd kept following her around the room as if his body refused to follow the dictates of his brain. Baser impulses ruled—impulses driven by the organ between his legs and the urgent need to claim what he'd once so desired.

That *had* to be the reason for his current fixation. He'd once been prepared to offer Safiyah everything—his name, his loyalty, his wealth. Now he had the opportunity to claim what he'd been denied.

Relief dribbled through him. It was good to have a sane explanation for this urgent attraction.

A powerful throb of anticipation pulsed through him. That kiss, brief as it had been, had proved the attraction was there, stronger than ever.

'What are you thinking?'

She repeated his own question, her eyes narrowed and her chin lifted, as if she'd read the direction of his thoughts and didn't like it. That surprised Karim. He'd long ago learned to hide his thoughts.

'Just thinking about my priorities when we get to Assara.' He paused. 'I'll instruct my lawyers to draw up the adoption papers with the marriage contract.'

'Really? I hadn't expected that so soon. Thank you.'

For the first time since they'd met again Safiyah actually approached him. The tight line of her beautiful mouth had softened and her eyes glowed. If Karim had needed any proof that she was motivated by love of her child, here it was.

He watched the slow smile spread across her face and felt a curious niggle inside. What would it be like to have someone—Safiyah, for example—look at him that way.

Not because he was doing something for the one she loved, but because she cared for *him*?

Blood rushed in Karim's ears as he stiffened and pulled back. Such fanciful thoughts were totally foreign. He was a grown man. He didn't need anyone to care for him. It was just curiosity about the loving bond between mother and child. Something he'd never experienced.

As a child he'd convinced himself that his mother loved him. He had fragmentary memories of being held in soft arms and sung to. Of playing with her in that rose-scented courtyard.

But those memories were wishful thinking. If his mother had loved either of her children she wouldn't have deserted them—left them to the mercies of the man who'd raised them. The man he'd thought of as his father had been irascible, impatient, and never satisfied, no matter how hard Karim had tried to live up to his impossible standards.

'Karim? What is it?' Safiyah had lifted her hand as if to touch his arm.

A white-hot blast of longing seared him. Unlooked-for. Unwanted. Because hankering after such things made him weak. He'd almost fallen for that trap once before with Safiyah. But he'd learned his lesson.

'Nothing. Nothing at all.'

He let his mouth turn up in a slow smile. The sort of smile he knew melted a woman's resolve. Safiyah blinked. Twice. Her lips parted and he saw her pulse pound in her throat.

'On the contrary. Everything is perfect.'

CHAPTER FIVE

KARIM LEFT HIS meeting in the Assaran palace torn between satisfaction and frustration. The interminable deliberation over legalities was complete. Agreement had been reached on all the important issues—including the provisions for Tarek and Safiyah.

And if some of the Assaran officials had been surprised that he, the incoming Sheikh, was the one ensuring the little Prince lost nothing as a result of Karim's accession, they'd quickly hidden it.

As for the red tape…

His homeland of Za'daq had its fair share, but Assara outdid it. They'd spent hours longer than necessary on minutiae. But Karim hadn't hurried them. Time enough to streamline processes after he became Sheikh.

But now, after hours hemmed in by nervous officials and nit-picking lawyers, he needed air.

He turned away from the palace's offices, past the broad corridor leading to the state rooms, and headed down towards the main courtyard where he guessed the stables were.

Emerging outside, Karim glanced at the lowering sun dropping towards the distant border with Za'daq. Purple mountains fringed the horizon and even here, on the coast, he registered the unmistakable scent of the desert.

His nostrils twitched and he inhaled deeply, though he

knew he was imagining that elusive scent. The desert was half a day's journey away. Yet the very air seemed familiar here, as it hadn't in Europe and North America. He felt more at home in Assara than he had in years there.

Karim smiled as he sauntered across the yard to the stables. In the couple of days since he'd agreed to come here his certainty had increased. He'd made the right decision.

But his smile faded as he registered the stable's echoing silence. The doors were shut and there was no sign of activity except in a far corner, where part of the stables had been turned into garages. There, a driver was busy polishing a limousine.

'The stables?' he said, when questioned. 'I'm sorry, sir, but they're empty. No one has worked there in years. Not since the last Sheikh's father's time.'

'There are no horses at all?'

Karim couldn't believe it. Assara was known for its pure-bred horses. Surely the Sheikh would have the finest mounts? Plus, Safiyah had virtually been born in the saddle. Riding was a major part of her life.

He remembered the first time he'd seen her. She'd been on horseback, and her fluid grace on that prancing grey, her lithe agility and the way she and the horse had moved as one had snagged his admiration. The sight had momentarily made him forget the reason he was visiting her father's stud farm, the horse he wanted to buy.

'Where does the Sheikha keep *her* horses?'

'The Sheikha, sir? I don't know of her riding or about any horses.'

Karim stared. Safiyah? Not riding? It was impossible. Once there'd been talk of her possible selection for the national equestrian team. He recalled thinking she'd never looked more alive than on horseback. Except when she was in his arms.

The memory curled heat through his belly, increasing his edginess.

Thanking the driver, he turned and entered the palace, heading for the royal suites. It was time he visited Safiyah anyway. The past couple of days had been taken up with meetings and he'd barely seen her.

Five minutes later he was admitted into her apartments. His curiosity rose as he entered. This was the first room he'd seen in the palace that looked both beautiful and comfortable rather than grandiose. The sort of place he could imagine relaxing after a long day. He liked it.

'If you'd like to make yourself comfortable, sir?' The maid gestured to a long sofa. 'I'll tell the Sheikha you're here.' She bobbed a curtsey and headed not further into the apartment, as he'd expected, but through the open doors into a green courtyard.

Instead of taking a seat Karim followed her, emerging into a lush garden full of flowering plants. Pink, white and red blossoms caught his eye. Fragrance filled the air and the swathe of grass curving amongst the shrubs was a deep emerald.

He paused, taking in the vibrancy of the place, so unlike the courtyards elsewhere in the palace, which were all symmetry and formal elegance. This was inviting, but casual, almost mysterious with its thick plantings and meandering paths.

The sound of laughter drew him forward. There was the maid, moving towards someone half hidden from view. Beyond her, on the grass, was a tumble of movement that resolved itself into a floppy-eared pup and a small boy. Giggles filled the air and an excited yapping.

Karim stepped forward and discovered the half-hidden figure was Safiyah, seated on the grass.

His gaze was riveted to his bride-to-be. In Switzerland he'd seen her cool and reserved, then later satisfyingly breathless in his arms. He'd seen her mutinous and imperious. But he hadn't seen her like this—relaxed and happy, with laughter curving her red lips.

For a moment something shimmered like golden motes in the late-afternoon light. A mirage of the past, when they'd enjoyed each other's company, gradually getting to know one another. Safiyah had laughed then, the sound sweet as honey and open as sunshine. Her laughter, her eager enjoyment of life, had been precious to someone like him, brought up by a man who had been at best dour, at worst irate, and always dissatisfied.

'Karim.'

Her eyes widened and the light fled from her expression. Stupid to mind that the sight of him dulled her brightness. It wasn't as if he wanted to share her laughter. He wasn't here for levity.

Safiyah said something and the maid moved towards the boy as if to scoop him up.

'No. Don't take him away.' Karim turned to Safiyah. 'Don't cut short his playtime because of me.'

It was time for him to meet the boy. Karim had agreed to be a father to him. The idea still elicited a confusing mixture of feelings and he'd berated himself more than once for acting as if on a whim where Tarek was concerned.

But it was no whim. The thought of the little Prince at the mercy of a ruthless man like Shakroun had struck a chord with Karim. He'd had to act. Nor could he rip the child's birthright away. Just as he hadn't been able to take the crown of Za'daq over Ashraf, though he'd been brought up solely for that purpose.

Besides, Karim knew what it was like growing up with the burden of royalty. The child needed a role model—one who understood that there was more to life than court protocol and politics. Karim would be that mentor.

An inner voice whispered that he hadn't been such a

good mentor to his younger brother…hadn't been able to protect him from his father's ire or bring much joy into his world. He vowed to do a better job with Tarek.

Safiyah rose in one graceful movement. Her long dress of deep amethyst slid with a whisper around that delectable body and Karim cursed his hyper-awareness of her. It had been like that since they'd arrived in Assara. No, since that kiss in Switzerland, that had left him fighting to mask his urgent arousal.

Karim drew a slow breath and forced himself to admit the truth. He'd been attuned to her from the moment she'd turned up in his hotel suite. She still had the power to unsettle him.

Safiyah murmured something to the maid, who melted back down the path.

'How kind of you to visit.'

Safiyah clasped her hands at her waist and inclined her head—the gracious Queen greeting a visitor. Except this visitor was the man who was about to save her country and her son. And he was going to become far more to her than a polite stranger, no matter how hard she pretended indifference.

Satisfaction banished his jab of annoyance at her condescension. Soon there'd be no pretence of them being strangers.

'The pleasure is all mine.'

He let his voice deepen caressingly. Her eyes rounded and he smothered a smile. Oh, yes. He was looking forward to a much closer relationship with Safiyah. Her attempts to keep him at a distance only fired his anticipation.

'I thought I'd take a ride, but discovered the stables empty.'

'My husband wasn't a rider.'

Karim watched her refold her hands, one over the other. Her mouth flattened, disguising those lush lips. Curiosity stirred. His nape prickled with the certainty that he'd hit on a subject she didn't want to discuss. Which made Karim determined to discover why.

Was her reaction a response to him or to the mention of her dead husband?

'But you are.'

He wasn't sure why he pressed the point, except that it was sensible to know the woman he was about to marry.

She lifted her shoulders but the gesture was too stiff to be called a shrug. 'I was.'

Karim lifted one eyebrow questioningly.

'I don't ride any more.'

The words were clipped and cool, but he sensed something beneath them. Something that wasn't as calm as the image she projected.

He waited, letting the silence draw out. Concern niggled. Had she had a bad fall? Had she been seriously injured? It would take a lot to keep the woman he'd once known away from her beloved horses.

Finally, with a tiny exhalation that sounded like a huff of exasperation, she spoke. 'Abbas didn't ride and he preferred that I didn't either.'

'Why?'

Karim shoved his hands in his pockets and rocked back on his feet, reinforcing the fact that he had plenty of time. Especially as he sensed Safiyah was reluctant to explain.

Equestrian prowess was a traditional part of a warrior's skills. It was unusual to find a ruler who didn't ride—especially as Assarans were proud of their fabled reputation as horsemen. The country was world-renowned for the horses it bred in the wide fertile valley along its northern border.

Safiyah darted a glance at the little boy and the puppy, now playing a lolloping game of chase. Was she checking they were okay or whether her son was listening?

'When I got pregnant I was advised not to ride. To keep the baby safe.'

Karim nodded. That he understood. But that had been years ago. There was more to this tale.

'And after the birth?'

A wry smile curved her lips. 'Only someone who hasn't gone through childbirth would ask that.'

It was tempting to be side-tracked by that smile, but Karim knew a diversion when he heard it. 'Not immediately, but in the years since your son was born. Why haven't you ridden?' A crazy idea surfaced. 'Did he forbid it?'

Karim knew by the sudden widening of her eyes that he was right. Sheikh Abbas had forbidden his wife to ride. But why?

Safiyah lifted her chin. There was no trace of her smile as she surveyed him with regal hauteur. That was something she'd learned only recently. The woman he'd known had been as fresh and unaffected as they came. Or, he amended, had given that impression...

'If it was known that I rode regularly I'd be expected to ride during royal processions and official gatherings. That was what royals have always done in the past. But...'

'But then you'd show up your husband if you were on horseback and he wasn't?'

A flush climbed her slender throat and she looked away. As if *she* were the one with an embarrassing secret.

'What happened? Did he have a bad fall? Is that what made him afraid to ride?'

The colour had seeped across her cheekbones now. 'It's not important. Abbas was beginning to modernise Assara. He saw no point in clinging to tradition. Travelling by car is quicker and more convenient.'

The words sounded like something she'd learned by heart. No doubt they'd been her husband's.

Karim felt something gnaw at his belly. Dislike.

He'd carefully not allowed himself to dwell on thoughts of Safiyah with her husband. He'd spent enough fruitless hours in the past, fuming over the way she'd dumped him so unceremoniously and then given herself to another bridegroom a mere five months later.

At the time the idea of Safiyah with another man, in his bed, giving him what she'd denied Karim, had been a special sort of poison in his blood.

But now his animosity was directed at Abbas.

Particularly as the possibility now arose that her defence of the dead man might be driven by love.

It hadn't occurred to Karim that Safiyah had *loved* her husband. There'd been no outward sign of it. On the contrary, her response to *him* had told him she didn't carry a torch for Abbas. No, ambition had been behind her first marriage, not love.

'Tradition matters if the people still value it.'

He read the flicker in her expression and knew that to many in Assara seeing their Sheikh on horseback *was* still important.

'And it matters that he stopped you from doing something you love just to save himself embarrassment.'

It was the action of a coward. But Karim kept the thought to himself. He was, after all, talking to the man's widow.

Something dark and bitter curled through his belly. He ignored the sensation, shifting his stance.

Safiyah curved her mouth into a smile that didn't reach her eyes. 'Well, you'll be able to fill the stables if you wish.' Before he could respond she looked at her watch. 'It's getting late. Time for Tarek to go to bed. If you'll excuse me…?'

'Introduce me—' Karim stopped, wondering. Did four-year-olds *do* introductions, or should he just get down on his haunches and say hello?

For the first time since he'd agreed to come here and take

on the kingdom he felt unsure of himself. He ignored his uncertainty and crossed the grass to where the child and dog lay, panting, after their game. The kid registered his presence, looking up, then up again, till a pair of brown eyes met his. Brown flecked with honey, just like his mother's.

Why that should affect Karim he didn't know, but he registered a thump in the vicinity of his ribs as that little face with those wide eyes turned to his.

'Tarek, I want you to meet...' Safiyah paused. Was she wondering how to describe him? Not father...not Sheikh yet.

'Hello. My name is Karim. I've come to live at the palace.'

The boy scrambled to his feet and, after swiping his dirty hands on the back of his shorts, stood straight and extended one hand. 'Hello. I'm Tarek ibn Abbas of Assara. It's a pleasure to meet you.'

Karim closed his palm around the tiny hand and gave it a gentle shake. He stared into the small, serious face regarding him so intently, as if looking for signs of disapproval.

With an audible whoosh of sound in his ears Karim found himself back in time, learning from a courtier the precise grades of greeting and which was suitable for royalty, for members of court, foreign dignitaries and ordinary citizens. He must have been about Tarek's age and he'd mastered the lesson quickly, since the alternative—disappointing his irritable father—hadn't been an option.

'The pleasure is mine, Prince Tarek.' Karim inclined his head over the boy's hand before releasing it.

The child nodded in acknowledgement but his eyes were already flicking back to the puppy chewing at his shoe. Tarek might be a prince but he was above all a little boy. And in that instant Karim was swamped by a determination to achieve at least one thing. To allow Tarek to have a childhood despite being royal.

Something Karim had never had.

He'd grown up with no time for idle play or cuddles. Instead there'd been constricting rules and a strict regimen devised to ensure he became a miniature copy of his father.

Seeing the yearning look on the boy's face as his royal training battled his inclination for fun, Karim smiled and squatted down. 'He's a fine-looking dog.'

In fact the boisterous pup was anything but beautiful. It had the long, silky tail and soft ears of a hunting dog but those short legs and nuggety body belonged to some other breed entirely.

Karim recalled the pure-bred hounds his father had kept, whose pedigree was as important as any other quality. Karim felt a surge of empathy with the mongrel pup and reached out to pat it—only to have it gnaw experimentally on his fingers.

'He likes you!' The last of Prince Tarek's gravity disintegrated as he threw himself down on the ground with his pet. 'He doesn't mean to hurt you,' he added earnestly. 'He bites people he likes.'

'I know. It's what puppies do.'

Karim was rewarded with a wide smile and responded with a grin.

'Do *you* have a dog?' the boy enquired.

Karim shook his head. 'I'm afraid not.'

'You could play with us if you like.'

He was surprised to find himself moved by the child's generosity. How long since he'd done something as simple as play with a dog? Or talk to a child?

'I'd like that, thank you.' He scratched the dog's spotted belly. 'What's his name?'

'Blackie. I picked it.'

Karim nodded. 'You picked well. Is he yours?'

'Yes. But he doesn't sleep with me.' The boy pouted, using rounded cheeks and outthrust lip to full advantage as his gaze slid reproachfully towards his mother. 'He *should* sleep in my bed. So I can look after him if he gets lonely in the night. Don't you think?'

Karim sensed Safiyah standing behind him, yet she said nothing. Was she waiting to see how he responded?

'Dogs need space, just like people do. I'm sure Blackie has a cosy bed of his own.'

'He certainly does,' Safiyah chimed in. 'Just down the hall. He sleeps so well that Tarek has to wake him up to play sometimes. Now, it's time to say goodnight. Tarek and Blackie need to go to bed.'

Karim watched the little boy struggle with the urge to argue. But eventually he got to his feet.

His eyes were on the same level as Karim's as he said, 'I like you. Come and play again.' Then, with a flickering look at his mother he smiled and added, 'Please.'

Tarek's mixture of royal imperiousness and friendliness appealed. Far more than the cautious, almost obsequious approaches Karim usually got from those eager to impress.

'I'd like that. Thank you,' Karim said again. He returned the smile with one of his own.

He'd enjoy spending time with little Tarek. For one thing, it would be a pleasant change. For as long as he could recall he'd been unable to trust that the people who tried to get close to him did so out of affection instead of for personal gain.

Safiyah bent to scoop the tired pup into her arms and take Tarek by the hand. Karim felt that all too familiar clench in his groin as her dress pulled over ripe curves.

Once she'd played up to him because she'd believed he could make her a queen. Now she'd come to him because she needed his protection.

Always because she wanted something from him.

Not because she wanted *him*.

It was a timely reminder. One he wouldn't forget.

But that didn't mean he couldn't enjoy the benefits of having Safiyah as his wife.

Suddenly the tedium and frustrations of the afternoon's long meeting disintegrated. Karim found himself looking forward to embracing his new life.

The vast, circular audience chamber was filled to the brim. Guests even outnumbered the stars of pure gold that decorated the domed ceiling of midnight-blue. The crush of people made Safiyah glad she was on the raised royal dais. Yet her heart still pounded as if she'd had to fight her way through the throng.

As of a few minutes ago, Karim had become Assara's ruler.

Thinking about it made her light-headed—with relief, she told herself, not nerves. Yet she kept her eyes on the crowd, not on the man further along the dais.

She had a perfect view of their faces, the VIPs of Assara, as they took turns to swear fealty to their new Sheikh. There were politicians, clan elders and powerful businessmen. Even the other men who'd hoped to be Sheikh.

Safiyah watched, her breath stalling, as the person before Karim bowed and backed away. Next in line was Hassan Shakroun. Shakroun's lips twisted unpleasantly, but that wasn't unusual. The man rarely looked content.

To her immense relief, when Karim had been proclaimed Sheikh there'd been no protest. Karim's swift acceptance of the crown meant Shakroun had had no time to act against him.

Now Shakroun moved forward and bowed perfunctorily, then backed away.

Safiyah sighed in relief. She'd done right. Shakroun had no reason now to harm Tarek. He was safe. It was Karim who had the power to make or break Tarek's future.

Despite his assurances, it was impossible not to wonder what sort of ruler he'd make, and what sort of father.

What sort of husband?

A jitter of nerves shot through her, churning her stomach. She breathed out slowly, forcing her heartbeat to slow.

As soon as the coronation ceremony was over their marriage would take place, and then Karim's formal adoption of Tarek.

What she'd give for her sister to be here. But, following tradition, there were no females in the room. Except her. Karim had made an exception to past practice by inviting her to attend the ceremony that would make him Sheikh.

Reluctantly she looked again at the centre of the dais. There, surrounded by the leaders of the Council, stood Karim, regal in pure white trimmed with gold. Even the *agal* encircling his headscarf was gold, a symbol of his new status.

He stood a head taller than the older men around him. Confident and commanding. His strong profile was proud, betraying no hint of doubt or weakness.

Tarek would grow up as the adopted son of the Sheikh. And she... She was destined to become once again wife of a sheikh.

Another breath, snatched into lungs that didn't seem to work.

Even the knowledge that this would be a marriage in name only couldn't ease the hammer-beat of her heart or the uneasy feeling that she'd acted against her better judgement.

Her second marriage of convenience. Her second marriage without love or real caring.

Safiyah pressed her palm to her abdomen as pain sheared through her. She'd learned to live with Abbas's indifference. Theirs hadn't been a close relationship, and in some ways there'd been relief in the fact they hadn't spent much time together.

Surely this new marriage would be similar. Karim's distaste had been clear after that kiss in Switzerland. *She'd* been the one swept away. He'd been as unmoved as one of those looming Swiss mountains. Her cheeks flamed at the memory.

And yet, this marriage *wouldn't* be like her one to Abbas. Then she'd been so miserable and lost that even going through the motions of marriage had been just one more burden. Dazed with grief over her father and her broken heart, nothing had mattered but doing her duty.

Now there was nothing to cushion her from the reality of her actions.

Her gaze returned to the arrogantly masculine profile of the new Sheikh. A riot of emotions roiled through her.

This marriage was going to be far worse than her first. She was marrying not a stranger, but the one man she'd ever loved. The man she'd yearned for with all her youthful heart.

She didn't love him any more. The very idea chilled her. Because doing so would make her impossibly vulnerable. But she'd cared for him once and felt sickened by the idea of living a pale imitation of the life she'd once hoped for.

Yet it was worse even than that. For though she didn't love him, and he was indifferent to her, Safiyah still wanted Karim as a woman wanted a man.

She desired him.

How was she to survive this marriage? Ignoring his indifference and the women he'd take into his bed? She didn't—

Suddenly the old men around the Sheikh shuffled back and that bronzed, handsome face turned. Safiyah felt the impact of that stare. It seemed as if his gaze bored straight past her blushing cheeks, past the sumptuous gown and jewels, deep into her aching heart.

The illusion strengthened when his eyes narrowed and

his nostrils flared, as if he sensed her doubts and the urge to flee which she had only just mastered.

But Safiyah was strong. Or she could pretend to be—even if she felt weak-kneed and terrified.

She lifted her chin and held that keen gaze like a queen.

CHAPTER SIX

'SAFIYAH.' KARIM FOUND himself crossing the dais to stand before her instead of simply summoning her with a gesture.

He heard the murmur of voices as people noted his action, and he didn't care. The previous Sheikhs of Assara might have moved for no one, but Karim would rule in his own way. He'd wanted to go to her from the moment she'd paced decorously into the room, like some exquisite medieval illumination come to life.

She glowed in jewel tones, her long dress of gold brocade revealing amber and red depths when she moved. The tiara of old gold and rubies turned the sensual woman he knew into a regal beauty. The matching chandelier earrings drew attention to the delicate line of her slender neck. Her air of shuttered stillness made him want to muss her hair with his hands as he tasted those luscious lips again and brought her to frenzied, rapturous life.

Drawing back from her passionate kiss, pretending to be unmoved by it, had been appallingly difficult. Fortunately pride and his once-bruised ego had come to the rescue.

'Your Majesty.'

She sank into a curtsey so low that the shimmering gown rippled across the floor around her like a molten lake. Head bent, she stayed there, awaiting his pleasure. But despite the profound gesture of obeisance there was an indefinable air of challenge about her.

This woman kept her own counsel and tried to maintain her distance. When he'd spent a little time with her and Tarek he'd been even more aware of the wall she'd built around herself.

He reached down and touched her hand, felt her flinch, and then, as he slid his hand around her wrist, the quick flutter of her pulse.

'You may rise.'

She did, but even so kept her eyes downcast. Anyone observing would see a beautiful queen, modestly showing respect for her new Sheikh. But Karim was close enough to read the swift rise and fall of her breasts and see the tiny tremors that ran through her.

Not so indifferent, my fine beauty, no matter how you try to hide it.

'You look magnificent.' His voice deepened in appreciation.

She lifted her eyes then. The velvety brown looked darker than usual, without the gold highlights he used to admire. They looked soul-deep and...worried? Despite his impatience, the idea disturbed him. What had she to worry about now he'd come to her rescue?

He told himself not to be taken in.

His feelings for her were too confused.

Once he'd been well on the way to being enchanted by Safiyah. He'd believed her gentle, honest and sweet. Then he'd wanted to hate her for deserting him.

Since meeting her again he'd experienced a mixture of distrust, anger, lust and a surprising protectiveness. Whatever else, she'd proved herself courageous when danger threatened her son. Or was she just grasping, scheming to retain her privileged position?

But marriage had been *his* idea, not hers.

He didn't trust her, didn't want to like her, and yet his hunger for her was tempered by reluctant admiration. It took guts for her to face him again, to consent to marry him and carry it off with such panache.

He lifted her hand and kissed it. A whisper of a kiss, yet he felt the resonance of her shock in his own body.

Want. Need. Hunger.

Soon they'd be assuaged.

'Come…' He smiled down at her, not bothering to hide his satisfaction. 'It's time for our wedding.'

Safiyah closed the door to her apartments behind her and sagged back, grateful for the solid wood supporting her spine. She felt drained. The ceremony hadn't taken long, but the celebrations had lasted hours. And that was just the first day. Tomorrow the celebrations continued—and the day after that.

Yet it wasn't the hours in heavy brocade and jewels, performing her royal duties, that had exhausted her. It was stress. The knowledge that she was now Karim's *wife*!

A sob rose and she stifled it, pushing away from the door, making herself walk into her rooms though every limb felt shaky.

It was a paper marriage. It didn't mean anything except that Tarek was safe. And that she'd have to keep on playing the public role of adoring, compliant spouse of a man who didn't give a damn about her.

Again that tangle of emotions rose, almost choking her. She swallowed, blinked back the heat glazing her eyes, and kept walking.

Usually her maid would be there, but Safiyah had known she wouldn't be able to face anyone and had dismissed her for the night. Now she half wished she hadn't. Just unpinning the tiara would take ages. But better to wrestle with it and her overwrought emotions alone.

At least she had practice in doing that. It seemed a lifetime ago that she'd had anyone she could lean on emotionally. Not since her mother had died when Safiyah was in her teens. She'd loved her father, but he'd never fully recovered from the loss of his wife. And her little sister had spent years battling her own demons of anxiety and depression, so Safiyah had supported her rather than the other way around.

As for Abbas…despite their physical intimacy there'd never been any question of sharing her feelings with him. He hadn't been interested. And life at the palace had isolated her from her friends.

She swung around, caught sight of herself in a mirror, all gold and jewels, and grimaced, feeling ashamed. She had so much. She had no right to feel sorry for herself.

Nevertheless, she turned on the music her sister had given her for her last birthday—a compilation of gentle tunes harmonised with wild birdsong and even the occasional sound of water falling. Rana said it helped to relax her and Safiyah had found the same.

She switched on a couple more lamps so the room felt cosy, unhooking the heavy earrings with a sigh of relief and placing them on the waiting tray in her dressing room. Her bangles followed—ornate, old, and incredibly precious heirloom pieces.

With each piece she imagined a little more of the weight lifting from her shoulders.

She lifted her hands to the tiara, turning towards the full-length mirror that took up one wall of the dressing space.

'Would you like help with that?'

The voice, smoky and low, rolled out of the shadows behind her.

Safiyah froze, elbows up, staring at the figure that had stepped into her line of vision in the mirror. Her pulse rocketed and the remnants of distress she'd been battling coalesced into a churning, burning nugget of fire in her abdomen.

Karim looked good—better than good. The traditional robes suited him, accentuating his height, the breadth of his chest and the purity of his strong bone structure that made his stern face so appallingly attractive. He'd discarded his headscarf and for some reason the sight of his close-cropped black hair after the formality of their wedding celebration seemed too…intimate.

As did the fact he was in her private rooms!

'Karim!'

Safiyah swung round, her arms falling to her sides. How long had she held them up? Her hands prickled with pins and needles. Her nape too, and then her whole spine as she met those hooded eyes. His stare was intense, skewering her to the spot and totally at odds with his relaxed stance. He leaned with one shoulder propped against the doorjamb.

Safiyah swallowed, then swiped her dry mouth with her tongue. Karim didn't move a muscle, but she sensed a change in him. The air crackled. The tingling along her backbone drove inwards, filling her belly with a fluttering as if a thousand giant moths flapped there, frantically trying to reach the glowing moon that hung in the night sky.

'What are you doing here, Karim?' Finally she collected herself enough to clasp her hands at her waist to conceal the way they trembled.

'I've come to see you, obviously.' He straightened and crossed towards her, making the room claustrophobically close. 'Turn around.'

'Sorry?' Safiyah gaped up at the face that now hovered far too close.

His expression gave nothing away. 'Turn around so I can help with the pins.'

'I don't need any help.'

Too late. He'd lifted his hands and she found herself encircled by the drape of snowy white fabric, deliciously scented with sandalwood and hot male. *Very* hot male.

Her cheeks flushed and something disturbing rippled through her.

Desire. Memory. The recollection of how she'd lost herself in his kiss.

He plucked at a pin, twisted another. 'Shh…don't fidget. Let me finish this, then we can talk.'

Relief cascaded through her. He wanted to talk. Probably about tomorrow's festivities. She was letting her unguarded responses get the better of her.

When they talked, the first item on her agenda would be to make it clear he couldn't stroll into her rooms whenever he felt like it. But she'd rather make her point when they were out in the sitting room. Having him in this very private space was too unsettling.

Safiyah drew a slow breath and nodded, wincing when his hold on the tiara stopped it moving with her.

'Sorry.'

Her eyes were on a level with his collarbone and she watched, bemused, the play of muscles in his throat. How could something so ordinary look…sexy?

'Wait. I'll turn.' Anything to give her breathing space.

But when she turned she was confronted with a mirror image of him looming behind her, his shoulders too wide, too masculine. Especially when the dance of his fingers in her hair felt like a deliberate caress.

He was surprisingly deft, making her wonder what experience he'd had in unpinning women's hair. Safiyah had no doubt he'd undressed plenty of women in his time. But, to her shock, she discovered having Karim undo her hair felt almost as intimate in its own way as sex had felt with Abbas.

She blinked, stunned at the idea, and found herself looking into a stare that sent fiery shivers trailing to a point deep inside her. That elusive place where, just once or twice, as

Abbas had taken his pleasure with her, there'd been a hint that she too might discover something more—

'There.'

Did she imagine Karim's voice was huskier? He lifted the tiara off with one hand, and Safiyah was about to thank him when he ploughed his fingers through her hair, dragging it down to her shoulders.

His eyes held hers in the mirror as he used his hand like a comb, spreading her hair around her shoulders. Each stroke was a slow, delicious assault on her senses.

Safiyah felt the stiffness ease from her neck and spine... detected an urge to lean into that stroking touch. Horrified, she stepped forward—so fast that her hair snagged on the ancient gold ring that had been placed on his finger at his investiture today. Her head was yanked back, but she welcomed the pain because it broke the spell.

'Sorry.'

He frowned and worked his hand free, during which time she took the tiara from his other hand. Then she moved away, replacing it in the velvet-lined box with the earrings and bangles.

Snapping the lid closed, she spun round. 'Shall we?'

She didn't wait for a response but preceded him out of the dressing room and back to the bedroom. She was on her way towards her sitting room when his words stopped her.

'Here's fine.'

'Here?'

She swung around. Karim stood midway between the dressing room door and the bed. There were no seats in the room apart from a long cushioned sofa.

'We'll be more comfortable in the sitting room.'

'Oh, I doubt that, Safiyah.'

That deliberate tone sent a shot of adrenalin through her already tense body.

Suddenly, as if a curtain had been yanked back, Karim's

expression was no longer impenetrable. She read a glitter in those eyes that was shockingly familiar. Safiyah recognised the look of a man with sex on his mind. She almost fancied she saw the flicker of flames in Karim's dark eyes. The tendons at the base of his neck stood proud, and though he made no move towards her there was a waiting stillness in his tall frame that unnerved her.

Involuntarily, Safiyah backed up a step. To keep him from reaching for her or to stop herself doing something foolish?

In that second of realisation she was torn between dismay and the need to throw herself into Karim's embrace and let him do whatever he wanted.

Because *she* wanted. She'd been on a knife-edge of frustrated desire since that kiss in Switzerland and she despised herself for it.

'No!' She felt her eyes widen as he frowned. 'We're not doing *that*.'

'*That?*' he murmured. 'How coy you are.'

His mouth curled at the corners as if he were amused. Damn him. As if he knew she didn't even want to think about sex with him, much less say it out loud. As if he knew how desperately she fought the desire to do more than talk about it.

Safiyah stiffened her spine. She might not have Karim's no doubt vast experience. But that didn't make her a fool or a push-over.

Her chin hiked up. 'You seem to forget this marriage is for political reasons.'

'So? That doesn't mean we can't enjoy the personal benefits.'

The word 'personal' was a rough burr that rubbed across her skin, making the fine hairs on her arms stand erect.

'Can you honestly tell me you don't want me?'

His words sucked the air from her lungs as she realised

he'd read her secret. Of course he had. He'd had to peel her off him to end that kiss in his hotel suite. The memory mocked her.

Karim crossed his arms over his chest. The gesture emphasised both his powerful frame and that annoying air of arrogance. And, to her consternation, his sheer, unadulterated sex appeal.

She tried to concentrate on his arrogance. Even Abbas at his most regal had never irritated her with just a look. Karim did it with merely a raised eyebrow and the knowing gleam in eyes that looked smoky with intent.

Their marriage wasn't about them as individuals, but he saw no reason to deny himself a little sexual diversion with his new spouse. She was here, he was bored, or he wanted to celebrate, or maybe he just wanted to amuse himself at her expense. In Switzerland he hadn't bothered to hide his disdain.

She planted her hands on her hips and paced a step nearer as hurt, fury and frustration coalesced. 'I'm not a convenience, here for your pleasure, Karim. We established before we married that I won't share my bed with you.'

The lingering hint of a smile on that long mouth stiffened. He shook his head, taking his own step forward so they stood almost toe to toe and she had to tilt her neck to look down her nose at him.

Safiyah knew better than to back away. He'd take advantage of any show of weakness. So she was close enough to read what looked like conflicting emotions as he spoke.

'Believe me, there's nothing *convenient* about this, Safiyah. As for what you said before we married...' he spread his hands wide '...you're allowed to change your mind.'

'You don't really want sex with me, Karim. You're just here to score a point. To amuse yourself. It's a power thing, isn't it?'

He was just reinforcing the fact that *he* was the one in

this marriage who had the power, not her. He might have been kind to Tarek but with her he was ruthless.

'You're not even attracted to me. You made that clear the day you came to my hotel suite.' She refused to let her voice wobble as she recalled his dismissal.

'I did?' His mouth lifted at one side, but it didn't quell the impact of that hungry stare.

The air thickened and her breaths grew shallow as she fought to tug in enough oxygen. Her insides clenched and she pressed her thighs tight together, trying to counteract the bloom of heat at her centre. How could she feel furious and aroused at the same time?

'Don't play games, Karim. You said it was an experiment that proved you weren't interested.'

'An experiment, yes. But the results were obvious. Like a match to bone-dry kindling. If I hadn't stepped away when I did we'd have had sex on the sofa.'

Safiyah was so stunned she couldn't find her voice. She went hot, then cold, as her brain produced an all too vivid image of them naked on that sofa. Those long arms holding her close, that muscular body cradled between her thighs…

A shiver ripped through her and his eyes turned darker when he saw it.

Suddenly Safiyah knew she was in real danger—not from Karim but from herself. How easy it would be to give in and say yes, despite her pride and the way he'd treated her.

'It didn't occur to you that I was experimenting too? That maybe you misread my curiosity for something more?' It was an outright untruth, but it was all she could think of to rebut him. 'If you think I pined for you for years you're wrong. I didn't.'

That, at least, was true. She hadn't let herself pine. She'd tried to excise what she felt for him—like amputating a limb, cutting herself off from emotion. It had been the only way to survive. Lingering on what might have been would have destroyed her as depression had almost destroyed her sister. For five years Safiyah had been emotionally self-contained, her only close relationships with Rana and Tarek.

'Of course you didn't pine for me. You had another prince to snare.'

The sneer in his tone was like a slap. As if she'd deliberately set out to lure either him or Abbas into marriage! But before she could snap out a rebuttal he leaned forward, invading her space, filling her senses with the tang of hot male skin, with pheromones that made her all but salivate with longing.

'You wanted me in Switzerland, Safiyah. We both know it.'

The words ground through her, making her shiver. 'And you want me now. Every time we get close I read it in your eyes, in your body.'

His gaze dropped to her aching breasts as if he could see the hard nipples thrusting towards him even through the heavy patterned fabric.

Safiyah shook her head. The thick hair he'd undone slipped around her shoulders. She wished it could conceal her totally. She wanted to hide where he couldn't find her. Where she wouldn't have to face the truth about herself. That she wanted Karim as she'd never wanted any other man. Still.

'You're imagining things, Karim.' She paused and swallowed hard. 'I don't want you.'

His steady stare should have unnerved her, but she refused to look away. She'd done what she had to in order to save her son. Now she'd do what she must to save her sanity. Sex with Karim would be the worst possible idea.

Yet when he took that last tiny step that brought him flush against her, his feet straddling hers, it wasn't disgust that made her breath hitch. They were both fully clothed, yet everywhere they touched—her breasts against his torso, her thighs against his—fire ignited.

'Prove it.'

The words were warm air on her superheated flesh.

'Kiss me and walk away.'

Safiyah's gasp only succeeded in pressing her breasts against him.

'I don't need to prove anything.' Holding that moss-green stare grew harder by the second. In her peripheral vision she saw that firm mouth, like a magnet dragging her gaze.

'One kiss and I'll leave—*if* you want me to.'

'Of course I do. I want…' Her words died as a warm palm cupped her cheek, long fingers channelling through her hair, creating sensations so delicious that despite everything her eyelids grew heavy.

His other hand didn't grab at her, didn't force her close. Instead it settled light as a leaf on her shoulder, then slowly slid down the outside of her arm, and down…down to her hand where her fingers trembled.

He'd promised no coercion and he kept his promise. But the compulsion welling within her to give in to him was almost overwhelming. Safiyah stifled a sob at the strain of withstanding this torture.

He captured her wrist with a surprising gentleness. It was as if he cast a spell that kept her rooted to the spot, breathless. Even when he raised her hand and she felt the press of his lips to her palm, the hot, lavish swipe of his tongue setting off swirling sparks inside her, his compelling gaze and her enthralled brain kept her where she was.

He planted her palm against his cheek. She felt the hot silk of his flesh and the tiniest hint of roughness along his jaw, where by morning he'd need to shave. Under his guidance her hand moved up to his hairline, and of their own volition her fingers channelled through the plush luxury of his hair.

So many sensations to absorb. Not least of which was the fascinating play of light…or was it darkness?… in Karim's eyes in response to her touch.

Safiyah's breath hissed as everything in her tightened. She had to move away, break this illusion of intimacy. Her brain told her that he was toying with her, but it felt so…

'We both want, Safiyah. And it will be good between us, I promise.' Again there was that curve of his mouth on one side, as if the flesh there were drawn too tight. 'Better than good. It will be—'

'Mama! Mama!'

A door banged and a woman's voice came from the next room. Then, before Safiyah could do more than turn her head, a small whirlwind shot through the door and landed against her legs.

'Tarek! What is it?'

She scooped him up and he clung, wrapping his arms and legs around her. He felt hot, and his face was damp as he burrowed against her. Automatically she murmured soothing words, clasping him tight.

'I'm sorry, madam—' Just inside the doorway the nanny jolted to a halt so suddenly she swayed. Her expression grew horrified as she took in Karim's presence and she sank into a deep curtsey. 'Your Majesty. My apologies, I didn't know—'

'No need for apologies,' Karim said. 'Clearly it's an emergency.'

'Just a nightmare, sir. I could have managed, but madam said—'

'You did right,' Safiyah assured her, rubbing a gentle hand over Tarek's skinny back and taking a few steps across to the bed, so she could sit down, holding her son close. 'I gave instructions to bring Tarek here if he needed me.'

It had been liberating, giving that order. When Abbas had been alive he'd demanded the nanny deal with any night-time upset without Safiyah, lest they were interrupted on a night he'd decided to visit his wife's bed.

'It is just a nightmare, isn't it?' Safiyah put her hand to Tarek's forehead as she rocked him in her arms. 'Not a temperature?'

The nanny rose, nodding. 'Just a bad dream, madam, but he kept calling for you.'

'Then he's in the right place now.'

It was Karim who spoke, drawing Safiyah's gaze. He didn't look as if he'd just been interrupted seducing his wife. She saw no impatience or annoyance. In fact he smiled as he told the nanny she could leave.

If it had been Abbas there'd have been cold fury and harsh words. Not because he'd been evil, but because he'd believed he was entitled to have his own way. That the world was ordered to suit *him*. He hadn't been deliberately cruel, but nor had he been sympathetic or used to considering others.

Safiyah looked from the departing maid to Karim, wondering how it was that this man, who'd also been raised to be supreme ruler, could react so differently. Where was the man who'd been so cold and distant in Switzerland?

Rueful eyes met hers and she felt again that pulse of awareness. It hadn't gone. His plans had merely been deferred. The realisation stirred excitement in her belly.

'How is he?'

'Calmer.' Tarek wasn't trembling now, though he still buried his head against her. Soon he'd be ready to talk. 'I'll keep him with me…settle him here.'

She waited for a protest from Karim but there was none. He walked to the bed and placed a large hand on her son's shoulder.

'Everything's going to be all right, Tarek. Your mother and I will make sure of it.'

To Safiyah's surprise Tarek lifted his head, sniffing, and nodded at Karim. Her husband smiled at the boy, then moved away.

'I'll leave you two to rest. Get a good night's sleep. It's going to be a big day tomorrow.'

Karim slanted her a look that made her toes curl. Then he drew a breath that made that impressive chest swell.

'You've had a lot to deal with, Safiyah. We'll discuss this later, when you've had time to adjust. After the wedding. But make no mistake: this is unfinished business.'

Then he turned on his heel and left, closing the door quietly behind him, just as if he hadn't turned her world inside out.

Already Tarek's eyes were closing. It seemed he didn't want to talk, just needed the comfort of a cuddle. Safiyah began singing a soft lullaby, but as she watched her son's eyes close and felt him relax she thought about what Karim had said.

There were two more full days of wedding celebrations. Two more days till Karim expected her to surrender to him. What was she going to do about that?

CHAPTER SEVEN

SAFIYAH EMERGED FROM the bathroom the next morning wrapped in her favourite robe. It was old, but it had been the last gift her mother had given her. The cotton was thin now, but the colour reminded her of the rare pale blue crocuses that grew in the mountains near where she'd grown up.

She hadn't worn it for ages because Abbas had expected her to dress in only the best. But he wasn't here to disapprove now, and in this last week especially Safiyah had found comfort in the memory of her mother.

Life had been turned upside down again and she was reeling from the impact. She hadn't been prepared for the tumult that was Karim's effect on her. She didn't want to trust him, kept remembering how badly he'd hurt her, yet at other times he seemed considerate, even kind. Like last night, when he'd put Tarek's needs before his own desire. It wasn't what she'd come to expect from men…from a husband. Karim confused her and made her feel things she didn't want.

Briskly, she rubbed her hands up and down her arms, banishing that little judder of residual awareness. She smiled at her waiting maid, then stopped abruptly.

'What's that?'

Her gaze fixed on the clothes spread out on the bed. She'd requested her long dress in shades of ochre and amber. Instead the fabric on the bed was an arresting dark lilac, embroidered with gleaming purple and lilac beads.

'Isn't it beautiful? The Sheikh has requested you wear this.'

Safiyah crossed to the bed, leaning down to stroke the fabric. The silk tunic was feather-light, the embroidery exquisite. It would be comfortable as she stood in the open air beside her new husband to receive the greetings of their people. The sunlight would glimmer off the rich decoration with each movement, subtly reinforcing her royal status as consort to the Sheikh.

'Are those trousers?'

Sure enough there was a pair of lightweight, loose-fitting trousers to wear beneath the long tunic. The style was often worn by women in the rural areas of her country, but Abbas had preferred her to wear dresses.

'They are, madam, and I've checked. They're exactly your size.' Her maid slid a sideways glance to her. 'Someone has been very busy making this for you.'

But why? Safiyah was quite capable of choosing her own clothes for royal events, and Karim didn't seem the sort to micromanage such details. But then, this second day of the joint coronation and wedding celebrations was an important one, during which they'd meet the people who had flocked to the capital from every province. Perhaps he was concerned about making the right impression. Wearing clothes that were a nod to the rural traditions of his new people wouldn't hurt.

'Very well.' She shrugged out of her robe.

But as the silk garments settled on her, drifting over her skin like a desert zephyr, Safiyah couldn't help but remember Karim's caress last night. He'd said things would be good, better than good, when she came to him.

If she came to him.

She hadn't agreed.

Yet.

* * *

Safiyah stepped out of the palace and into the main courtyard, only to hesitate on the threshold. There, instead of a gleaming entourage of black limousines, was a bustle she'd never seen within the royal precinct. The scene was alive with movement, the jingle of metal on metal and the clop of hoofs on cobblestones. The rich tang of horse and leather filled her nostrils and something within her lifted like a bird taking flight.

The place was full of riders. Two standard-bearers carrying the turquoise and white flag of Assara were mounted at the head of the line. Behind them, on snorting sidestepping horses, were elders and clan leaders—a who's who of Assara, all looking confident and fiercely proud.

Safiyah thought of Karim's words when he'd learned that Abbas had ditched the equestrian gatherings so loved by his people. It was clever of him to reinstate them, for clearly this was what he'd planned.

'Safiyah.'

As if conjured by her thoughts, there he was, striding towards her, magnificent in pale trousers, boots and a cloak the colour of the desert sands. He had a horseman's thighs, flexing powerfully with each step. The fact she'd noticed sent a tremor through her.

Her stomach dived. How was she supposed to resist him when her body betrayed her this way? Her galloping heartbeat told its own story.

'Karim.'

She saw the gleam of anticipation in his eyes. Clearly he was looking forward to this. Yesterday he'd been solemn and proud, as befitted a newly made monarch. Today his eyes danced.

'You look magnificent.'

His smile was a slow spread of pleasure across his face

that did crazy things to her insides. He took her hand, lifted it and stepped back, as if to get a better view.

For one mad moment she felt that glow of anticipation was for her. Then sense reasserted itself.

Karim had more important things on his mind than the wife he'd married for purely political reasons. Like establishing his mark on the country. Making an impression not only on the great and the good, but on the ordinary people. Which was why he planned to ride out on horseback, as the Sheikhs of Assara had done for centuries.

'That's why you sent the trousers.' Belatedly it dawned on her. 'You want me to ride with you.'

As if on cue a groom led forward two horses. A magnificent grey for Karim and a chestnut mare with liquid dark eyes for her. Safiyah saw the creature and was torn between love at first sight and disappointment that all Karim's excitement was for the success of his plan.

It had been madness to imagine he was pleased to see *her*, personally. She was his convenient wife. Not good enough to marry for her own sake—he'd made that painfully clear years before—but useful to win the people's acceptance.

Safiyah slipped her hand from Karim's, ignoring the twitch of his dark eyebrows at the movement. 'You could have warned me.'

'Warned you?'

'That I'd be riding.' Clearly she wasn't important enough to be informed of his plans. She felt as if she was the last to know. This procession had clearly taken a lot of preparation.

Karim stepped closer, blocking out the stable hand waiting at a discreet distance. 'I thought you'd enjoy the surprise.'

Safiyah's eyes widened. He'd thought about what she'd *enjoy*? She shook her head. This equestrian parade was a PR exercise. Not to please her.

Yet the fact he'd bothered to consider how she'd feel about it was unexpected. Disturbing. She wasn't used to that. What did it mean?

'You don't believe me?' His eyebrows lifted and his chin too, in an expression of hauteur.

'I'm just surprised.' And bewildered.

His expression softened a little. 'Pleasantly so?'

Silent, she nodded.

'Good.'

For a moment Safiyah thought he'd say more. Instead Karim swept her once again with his gaze and it was all she could do not to blush like a virgin. For there was something about his expression that made her think not of the show he was putting on for the populace, but of how he'd stared at her last night. As if he'd wanted to devour her on the spot.

The hubbub died away till all she could hear was the quick pulse of her blood in her ears.

'Mama!'

She swung around as a small figure emerged in the doorway from the palace. Tarek, wearing his finest clothes, hurtled into her arms. Safiyah caught and lifted him, hiding her surprise.

'Did you come to see all the excitement, sweetie?'

He nodded and clung to her.

'He's come to take part in today's festivities,' Karim said. 'I want the people to see that he hasn't been shunted aside.'

That made sense to Safiyah. And it was in Tarek's own interests. It was a clever move that would help both Karim and her son. But, again, she hadn't been consulted.

Although had she really expected that Karim might discuss his plans with her when Abbas never had? Once more she could only obey and play the role demanded of her. It was stupid to feel disappointed that nothing had changed.

'What is it, Safiyah? You look troubled.'

Karim's low voice reminded her how dangerous he was, how much he saw. For she was wearing what she thought of as her 'royal' face. A mask she'd perfected over the years to hide her feelings. It disturbed her to think Karim could see past it.

She shifted Tarek higher. Her son was looking wide-eyed at the horses.

'He's never even seen a horse close up before. He can't ride. It's too much to expect him to be in this procession. It's far too dangerous.'

She refused to let Karim put her boy in danger for the sake of appearances, even if his word *was* law. She'd spent years being seen and not heard, but when it came to Tarek's wellbeing she refused to submit meekly any more.

For a long moment her new husband considered her. When he spoke his words were for her alone. 'You don't think much of me, do you, Safiyah?'

His eyes flashed annoyance. Yet for some reason she wondered if that anger hid something else.

Before she could respond another figure emerged from the palace.

'Rana!' Safiyah couldn't believe her eyes. Her sister... here? Her heart squeezed and her eyes prickled. She opened her mouth to say something but no words emerged.

Safiyah looked up at Karim, who was surveying her from under lowered brows, his crossed arms making him looking particularly unapproachable. As if the man who'd stirred her blood with that one appraising look just moments ago had never been.

Yet he, surely, was the man responsible for her sister's presence. Gratitude and a sudden flood of happiness quenched her indignation.

'Your Majesty.' Rana sank into a deep curtsey and Safiyah watched, stupefied, as Karim took her sister's hand and raised her, bestowing upon her a smile that was all charm.

'It's a pleasure to meet you, Rana. I'm glad you could come to support your sister and your nephew today.'

Safiyah looked from her sister to Karim. What was going on? Assaran royal weddings did *not* include female witnesses, even if the bride had no living male relatives. Safiyah had been the only woman at yesterday's ceremony. Nor were female members of the bride's family invited to the royal events in the days that followed. Safiyah had got through the interminable festivities of her first marriage unsupported except for the maid who'd attended her when she retired to her room.

Before she could ask for an explanation a harassed-looking steward came forward and murmured something to Karim, drawing him away.

'Surprise!' Rana kissed Safiyah on the cheek and Tarek on the forehead, her gentle smile lighting her face. 'Your husband invited me to the capital for the next two days.' Rana dropped her voice. 'You didn't tell me he was so nice. So thoughtful.' She paused, chewing her lip. 'I did wonder if you really wanted this marriage. It's happened so quickly.'

Safiyah could only be grateful that Rana didn't know about the history between her and Karim. Then she'd *really* have her doubts.

'I definitely wanted it, Rana.'

Her sister nodded. 'For Tarek's sake. But…' she paused '…maybe for your own too?'

Safiyah swallowed hard and managed a noncommittal smile. Now wasn't the time for explanations. Karim had already proved himself capable of protecting his new position and his new son. That was all that mattered. His attention to detail today was all geared towards shoring up public approval. Even down to having the Prince accompanied by his aunt instead of a nanny.

Karim was presenting the picture of a united, stable family to the nation.

What other reason could he have for making these arrangements?

'It's wonderful to see you, Rana.' Safiyah leaned in and cuddled her sister with one arm while holding Tarek on her hip. An upsurge of emotions blindsided her, catching at her throat.

She wasn't used to having someone by her side. Strange, too, to realise how much she needed that support. The last days had been a rollercoaster of emotional shocks.

Tarek wriggled in her hold. 'Down, Mama. I want to see the horses.'

'He's a chip off the old block,' Rana said. 'Once he gets a taste for riding you won't be able to keep him away from the stables. Just like you and me.'

Warmth swelled in Safiyah's chest at her sister's smile. They'd both ridden as soon as they could walk, like their father before them.

'Later, Tarek. If you're a good boy you can pat one of the horses later.' For now Karim was striding back towards them and the last of the riders were swinging up onto their mounts. 'It's time for you to go with Auntie Rana.'

But Tarek wasn't placated. He was going to argue. His bottom lip protruded.

'Here. Let me.'

Long arms reached for her boy. Karim's hands brushed against her as he took her son.

She didn't know what stunned her more. The ripple of sensation where Karim's hard hands had touched her arms and, fleetingly, the side of her breast. Or the sight of him holding Tarek. The way a father would.

Safiyah frowned. She couldn't recall the last time Abbas had held his son. For an official photo, most probably.

Karim caught the disapproving scrunch of Safiyah's forehead and turned away, anger flaring.

What was wrong with the woman? Didn't she trust him enough even to hold her precious son?

She trusted him enough to marry him, yet now she was fighting a rearguard action to keep a distance between them.

Karim had taken time to consider how to make these intense days of celebration easier for her. He'd gone out of his way to bring her sister here, and to involve Tarek in the event to shore up the legitimacy of his future claim. He'd even organised that whisper-soft concoction of a riding outfit that made Safiyah look even more beautiful and impossibly seductive.

Had he received any thanks? Only from her sister. From Safiyah—nothing at all. Not even a smile.

So much for gratitude.

But Karim shouldn't have expected gratitude. The woman had abandoned him when she'd discovered the truth of his birth. She only accepted him now because he could salvage her royal position and protect her child.

Wrenching his thoughts away from Safiyah in beaded silk, he focused on the child in his arms. Tarek stared up at him with big brown eyes, his bottom lip quivering.

Maybe Karim shouldn't have swooped in and grabbed the child, but it seemed better to head off a tantrum than have the boy yowling through the parade.

'You want to meet a horse, Tarek?' He smiled encouragingly at the child and felt inordinately pleased when he received a grave nod. 'I'll hold you up high so you can pat one. Would you like that?'

He read the boy's excitement and for a second was

wrenched back to those rare moments in his childhood when he'd managed to steal time out with his little brother. Ashraf's eyes had glowed in just that way.

Karim walked up to the groom holding the reins of his mount and Safiyah's.

Automatically he turned towards the mare, as the smaller and more docile. But Tarek shook his head. 'This one.' He looked up at the dancing grey stallion.

Karim shrugged. The boy had pluck, that was for sure, if this really was the first time he'd got close to a horse. He'd have thought a beginner would be drawn to the mare, standing sedately. But Karim would keep him safe.

'This is Zephyr,' he murmured, and the grey flicked his ears forward, then huffed out a breath through flared nostrils.

Tarek giggled as the horse's warm breath brushed his face and hands. The horse's head reared back and Karim spoke to it in an undertone, reassuring it as he reached up to scratch near its ear.

'You can't be scared of Tarek, surely now? A big strong fellow like you?'

Again Tarek giggled, suddenly lunging forward in Karim's hold, trying to reach the horse.

'Not like that.' Karim hauled the child back. 'Give Zephyr a chance to know you. You have to sit quietly so as not to scare him. Put out your hand like this and let him sniff you.'

'It tickles!'

But to his credit the boy didn't squirm, even when Zephyr, with a sideways look at Karim, pretended to nibble the little Prince's sleeve.

The child gasped at the wet stain. Worried brown eyes met Karim's and once more he was reminded of his kid brother, this time after he'd been summoned before their disapproving father.

'I'm not supposed to get dirty. Papa says—'

'I know, but the rules have changed,' Karim said quickly, ignoring a moment's discomfort.

The child's dead father was beginning to remind him too much of the ever-demanding Sheikh who'd raised him. Karim recalled constant childhood lectures on his appearance, his manners, his attitude and even the way he walked. And that had been before the old man had got started on his studies.

'Don't worry, Tarek. It will dry quickly and no one will notice.' He paused. 'Do you want to know a secret?'

Solemnly the boy nodded.

'It's more important to be happy than to be clean.' Deliberately he looked furtively over his shoulder and pressed his finger to his lips. 'But don't tell anyone I said that. It's a royal secret.'

Tarek giggled, and Karim felt the strangest flutter in response. Even knowing it was the right thing to do, Karim had had qualms about adopting the boy. His experience of kids was limited. He was still learning how to interact with his little nephew on his rare visits to Za'daq. But Karim was determined to do right by Tarek—which meant taking time to build a relationship with the boy.

Finally Zephyr consented to be introduced, bending his head gracefully so the child could rub his palm over the grey's long nose.

'He smells funny.'

'Not *funny*,' Karim amended, watching, bemused, as the most highly strung horse in the city consented to the child's rough pats. Clearly the little Prince had his mother's knack with animals. 'That's how horses smell.'

'I like it.'

Tarek beamed up at him and Karim was surprised at how much he was enjoying the child's pleasure.

Karim caught movement in his peripheral vision and saw the steward scowling at his watch.

'Okay, Tarek. It's time for you to go with your aunt.'

The boy nodded enthusiastically and it was the work of a moment to settle him in the car next to Rana. When Karim turned back towards the waiting horses it was to find Safiyah watching him, her expression serious.

What now? Was she going to complain about him holding her son? She'd have to get used to it. Tarek was officially *his* son now too.

The idea elicited a welter of unfamiliar emotions.

'Ready, Safiyah?' He made to walk past her, heading to where their mounts stood.

'Yes, I...'

Her words trailed off and Karim paused. It was unlike Safiyah to hold back. She said what she thought—particularly when she disapproved. He was sick of her disapproval.

Repressing a sigh, he turned. 'What is it? It's time we started.'

Their route was to take a circuitous route through the city. It would be at least an hour before they arrived at the open-air venue where the celebrations would commence.

Her eyes met his, then swung away. Yet in that instant Karim was surprised to discover not anger but uncertainty. He took in her heightened colour and the dimple in her cheek and realised she was gnawing the inside of her mouth.

She moved closer, her hand hovering for a moment over his before dropping away. His flesh tingled as if from her touch.

'Thank you, Karim. You were so good with Tarek. Not stern or disapproving.' She smiled tentatively. 'It's more than I expected and I appreciate it.'

It was on the tip of his tongue to say of course she should expect people to treat her boy well. Except he recalled what

Tarek had said about his father. And how much he sounded like the man who'd raised Karim. Sometimes common courtesy and kindness to children weren't the norm.

Had that coloured Safiyah's view of Karim? The thought snagged in his brain. Maybe that explained some of the anomalies he'd noted in her behaviour.

It also made him wonder about her relationship with her first husband...

'I told you. I aim to do my best for the boy.'

If his tone was gruff she didn't seem to notice. She nodded, but didn't move. Harnesses jangled nearby yet still Karim waited, knowing there was more.

'I wanted to thank you, too, for bringing Rana here.' The words spilled out in a breathless rush. 'It was the most wonderful surprise. I...' She paused and looked down at her hands, clasped tight before her. 'I can't tell you how much it means to me to have her here.'

Safiyah lifted her head and her gaze met his. Karim experienced that familiar sizzle, but this time her curious expression—a mix of joy and nerves—didn't just ignite the accustomed flare of sexual anticipation. It made some unidentified weight in his chest turn over. The sensation was so definite, so unique, it held him mute.

For a long moment—too long—Karim felt the deep-seated glow of wellbeing he'd known only once in his life. In the days when he'd believed Safiyah to be a sweet, adoring innocent. But, despite her pretty speech of thanks, those days were dead. It was important he remembered that.

He nodded briskly and turned towards the groom, gesturing for him to bring the horses. They'd delayed longer than planned. It was time to ride out.

Suddenly Karim was itching to be gone, to be busy with his new work, his new people. Not second-guessing Safiyah's motives or his own feelings. He didn't have time for feelings—not personal ones. He wasn't here for old times' sake. He was here to rule a nation.

Yet when another groom approached, to help Safiyah into the saddle, Karim shook his head and offered his own clasped hands for her foot, tossing her up into the saddle. It was hardly an intimate caress. Just a fleeting touch of leather on skin. Yet the air between them shimmered and thickened as she looked down from the saddle and those velvet eyes met his. They'd darkened now, all trace of gold highlights disappearing. Her gaze felt intimate and full of promise.

Was it genuine or fake?

Marrying Abbas's widow and adopting his child had never been a straightforward proposition. Yet he hadn't realised how difficult it would be. For, despite years of experience in distancing himself from entanglements, this felt...personal. And complicated.

Karim had walked into a throne but also into a family. Into a place full of feelings and shadowy hints of past relationships that still affected Safiyah and Tarek today.

Suddenly the work of ruling Assara seemed easy compared with playing happy families.

Yet there was one aspect of family life Karim looked forward to with searing anticipation.

Bedding his wife.

CHAPTER EIGHT

'THANK YOU.' SAFIYAH nodded to the maid who was turning down the bed. 'That's all for tonight.'

With a curtsey the woman left. Instantly Safiyah put down her hairbrush and shot to her feet. She was too restless to sit.

Each passing day had fed the awful mix of anticipation and dismay that had taken root inside her. The three days of public celebrations had passed in a whirl of colour, faces and good wishes. At the end of it, almost swaying with exhaustion and nerves, Safiyah had prepared herself for a showdown with Karim.

He'd said he'd come to her when the wedding was over. To claim his marital rights. As if she were his possession, to do with as he wished.

Inevitably the idea had stirred anger. Yet if she were totally honest it wasn't just anger brewing in her belly.

But Karim hadn't come to her room on the final night of the celebrations.

Nor had he in the ten days that had passed since the end of the festivities.

Ten days!

Each night she'd prepared to face him and each night he'd failed to show.

He'd clearly changed his mind about his demand that

she sleep with him. Or maybe he hadn't been serious at all—had just wanted to watch her squirm.

What had she done to make him despise her so much?

Safiyah felt her thoughts tracking down that well-worn trail, but she refused to head there again. Instead she crossed the room, hauling off her robe and nightgown as she went, tossing them onto the bed. Seconds later she'd pulled on trousers and a shirt. Socks and boots.

She'd had enough of being cooped up with her thoughts. Her sister had gone home after the wedding and Safiyah, always careful not to burden Rana, had smiled and sent her off rather than beg her to stay. How she wished she had someone to talk to now.

What she needed was to get out. At least here in the summer palace, just beyond the outskirts of the capital, she had the means to do just that. For her lovely chestnut mare, a wedding gift from Karim, was stabled downstairs.

To anyone who cared to enquire, the Sheikh and Sheikha had begun their delayed honeymoon today. The small, secluded summer palace was close enough to the city for Karim to be on hand should anything significant need his attention, but the location between two idyllic beaches was totally private—perfect for newlyweds.

If the newlyweds had been at all interested in each other!

She hadn't seen Karim since they'd arrived. He'd headed straight to his office, trailed by a couple of secretaries, leaving Safiyah, Tarek and his nanny to settle into their rooms.

With a huff of annoyance Safiyah decided she'd rather be with her horse than stewing over whether Karim would deign to visit her. For ten days she'd been torn between anticipation—wanting to cut through this unbearable tension that ratcheted ever tighter—and dismay that finally she would give in to what she could only think of as her weakness for her necessary husband.

Twenty minutes later she was astride her mare as they

picked their way down the path to a long, white sand beach that shimmered in the early-evening light. Once clear of the palace and the protests of the groom, who had been dismayed that she chose to ride alone and bareback, Safiyah drew in a deep breath. The scent of the sea mingled with the comforting aroma of horse, lightening her spirits.

After all, there were worse things than a husband who didn't want sex and left her completely alone.

Safiyah shuddered, remembering the avid way Hassan Shakroun had eaten her up with his gaze in the days following Abbas's death. The idea of his fleshy paws on her body was almost as horrible as the thought of Tarek's safety being in his control.

Marriage to Karim had been the only sensible option. Tarek was protected and she… Well, she'd survived one loveless marriage and she could do it again. She'd happily live without sex. A marriage on paper only was what she'd stipulated. She should be glad Karim didn't want more.

Safiyah squashed the inner voice that said perhaps there was more to sex than she'd experienced with Abbas. Perhaps with another, more considerate lover, there might even be pleasure.

'Come on, Lamia,' Safiyah whispered to her mount. 'Let's go for a run.'

They were halfway down the beach when the sound of thunder reached her. It rolled along the sand behind her. Safiyah looked up but the sky was filled with bright stars, no sign of clouds. Besides, this noise kept going—a rumbling that didn't stop.

Pulling back on the reins, Safiyah looked over her shoulder. Instantly she tensed. Galloping towards her was a tall figure on a grey horse. An unmistakable horse and an unmistakable man.

Karim.

Together they looked like a centaur—as if Karim were

part of the big animal. Their movements were controlled, perfectly synchronised and beautiful. Yet the urgency of their sprint down the beach snared Safiyah's breath.

A frisson of excitement laced with anxiety raced up her spine to grab at her nape and throat.

There was nothing to fear from Karim. Only from herself and the yearning he ignited in her. Yet she couldn't shake her atavistic response. The instinct to flee was overwhelming. She was desperate to get away from this man she hadn't been able to escape even in her thoughts. He crowded her, confronted her, made her feel things she didn't want to feel. Even after ten days of waiting for him to come to her she found she wasn't ready to face her weakness for him.

Safiyah turned and urged her horse faster, first to a canter and then, as the thunder of hoofbeats closed in, to a gallop. The mare leapt forward and Safiyah leaned low, feeling her hair stream behind her as they raced away, exultation firing her blood.

But they weren't fast enough. Even over the sound of Lamia's hooves and her own heartbeat Safiyah heard the grey close in. Each stride narrowed the gap.

Her breath was snatched in choppy gasps. Her pulse was out of control. Still she sped on, desperate to escape her pursuer and all he represented. The man who threatened her not with violence, but because he'd awoken a need inside her that wouldn't let her rest.

He'd stolen her peace.

She had to get away. To preserve her sanity and the last of her self-respect.

Eyes fixed on the end of the beach, and the narrow ribbon of track that rose from up to the next headland, she wasn't aware of how close he was till a dark shadow blocked the silver of the sea and the thunder was upon her, filling her ears and drumming in her chest.

Even then Safiyah wouldn't give in. If she could get up on to the headland track before him—

It wasn't to be. One long arm snaked out and grabbed her bridle, then they were slowing, her mare easing her pace to match that of the stallion.

Safiyah's heart hammered. Her flesh prickled all over as the fight-or-flight response still racketed through her.

Finally they came to a halt in the shadow of the headland. Safiyah's blood pumped too fast and her breath was laboured. Each sense was heightened. The mingled scents of horse, sea salt and hot male flesh were piquant in her nostrils. The brush of Karim's leg against hers unleashed a storm of prickling response.

She stared at the sinewy strength of Karim's hand and wrist, clamped like steel on her reins. The silence, broken only by the rough breathing of the horses, grew louder.

'What the hell did you think you were doing?' The words sliced like a whip. Karim's eyes glittered diamond-hard even in the gloom.

Safiyah sat straighter, refusing to be intimidated. 'Going for a ride. Alone.' Was he going to take issue with that? After the thrill of being allowed to ride again for the first time in years, it was too much.

'You were heading straight for the rocks.' He sounded as if he was speaking through gritted teeth.

'You think I couldn't see them?' She shook her head, too annoyed to be quelled by the warning jut of his arrogant jaw. 'I was about to take the track up the headland.'

Karim's grip tightened on the reins and her horse sidled, pushing Safiyah closer to the big, glowering form beside her.

'Not at that speed. You'd break your neck.'

Safiyah glanced towards the pale track. This time the route didn't look quite so easy. Yet she refused to explain the urgent impulse to escape at any cost. She knew it would only reveal the fear she'd vowed to hide from Karim. That if she wasn't careful he'd overwhelm her and all her hard-won lessons in self-sufficiency.

She'd learned to cut herself off from the thousand hurts of a casually uncaring husband. She couldn't afford to lose that ability now when she most needed it.

'I'm more than capable of deciding where I ride. I don't need you dictating to me.'

A sound like a low growl emanated from Karim's throat, making the hairs on the back of her neck stand up. She'd never heard anything so feral. Karim had always been the epitome of urbanity, always in control.

'Do you have a death wish? What about Tarek? How would he cope if you broke your neck up there?'

Red flashed behind her eyes. 'Don't you bring Tarek into this!'

How dared he accuse her of being an irresponsible mother? Her mouth stretched into a grimace and her belly hollowed as she thought of the sacrifice she'd made for her son. Giving up her freedom for his sake by yoking herself to a man who disliked her.

Fulminating, Safiyah released the reins and vaulted from her horse.

'Where do you think you're going?'

Safiyah set her jaw and stalked away. Let him work it out for himself.

She'd only taken half a dozen steps when a hard hand captured her wrist, turning her to face him. He towered above her, imposing and, though she hated to admit it, magnificent.

'Don't turn your back on me, Safiyah.'

His voice was soft but ice-cold. It sent a shiver scudding across her skin. Even Abbas at his most imperious hadn't affected her like this.

Karim's hold was unbreakable. She'd look ridiculous

trying to yank her hand free. Instead she chose defiance cloaked in a façade of obedience.

She sank to a low curtsey, head bowed. 'Of course, *Your Majesty*. How remiss of me to forget royal etiquette.'

She heard a huff of exasperation and for a second his hand tightened around hers. Then, abruptly, she was free.

'Don't play with me, Safiyah. It won't work.'

She rose, but found Karim had stepped right into her space. They stood toe to toe, her neck arching so she could look him in the eye. She couldn't fully decipher his expression but saw enough to know she'd pushed him dangerously far.

Good. It was time someone punctured that ego.

'I'll get the horses.'

She made to move but he caught her upper arms. His clasp wasn't tight but for some reason Safiyah couldn't break away.

'Leave them. They won't go anywhere.' He paused. 'Why did you run, Safiyah? You knew it was me.'

She shrugged. 'I wanted a gallop.'

'Don't lie.' Gone was the icy contempt. In its place was a piercing intensity that probed deep.

'I'm not—'

'Was it because of this?'

Before she had time to register Karim's intention he hauled her up onto her toes. His head swooped low and his mouth crashed onto hers. Safiyah felt pressure, tasted impatience and hurt pride.

His anger fuelled hers, made it easier to withstand him. Even so, her body quaked with rampant need from being pressed up against his hard frame.

She just had to hang on a little longer, till he grew tired of this and pushed her away. He was angry. He didn't really want her.

Except even as she thought it everything changed.

Those hands wrapped over her arms turned seductive as they slid around her back. One slipped up into her loose hair, tangling there possessively and cradling her skull as he bent her back. His other hand skimmed her hip bone, then moved to cup her bottom. His fingers tightened as he pulled her up against a ridge of aroused flesh so blatantly virile that she gasped.

That gasp was her mistake. It gave Karim access to her mouth, where he delved deep, evoking shuddery thrills of excitement.

Safiyah told herself she shouldn't want this. Shouldn't want *him*. Not the dark coffee taste of him, not his sea and sandalwood scent, not that honed body. And especially not the tight, spiralling feeling low inside as he pressed against her, his erection a blatant male demand.

Yet there was no escape. Because already her fingers clenched into the soft cotton at his shoulders, digging into taut muscle so she felt the bone beneath. Safiyah tried to make herself let go, but her body acted on instincts that had nothing to do with self-preservation.

Karim murmured something against her lips that might have been her name. She couldn't hear it, just felt it as a vibration in her mouth. Then he kissed her harder, and she clung to him as everything spun away in an explosion of sensual delight.

When she could think again it was to find his hand sliding under her shirt to close over her breast. Her knees wobbled as, instead of a hard, crushing hold, she felt his touch gentle. Her breath hissed out as one finger traced narrowing circles around her silk-covered breast till he reached a nipple pouting with need.

Safiyah trembled at the pleasure of Karim's touch. Even the way he moulded her breast in his hand seemed designed to please her as much as him. The rush of moist heat between her legs surprised her. How could she feel like this when she didn't want him?

But you do, Safiyah. You've wanted him for weeks. For years.

It was the knowledge she'd tried to avoid. But denial was impossible as she shook in his arms. Only the support of his embrace held her upright.

As if reading her thoughts Karim broke the kiss, in the same movement scooping her up into his arms. There was something shocking about being held that way, reliant totally on him, curled against that broad, powerful chest as he strode towards the inky shadows beneath the cliffs.

Her eyes widened as she realised the most shocking part was how much she revelled in it. How the coiling twist of heat between her legs grew to a pulsing, urgent throb.

Safiyah caught a glimpse of their horses grazing at the edge of the beach. Then the world tilted as Karim lowered her to cool sand. He knelt above her, the star-quilted sky behind his head, his shadowed face unreadable.

For a second the idea infiltrated that she should stop this. She'd come here to get away from Karim. But only for a second. This…whatever this was…was unstoppable, like the surge of the tide or the rise of the moon.

Karim's knees were astride her thighs, his heat warming her through her trousers as deft fingers worked the buttons of her shirt undone. Safiyah reached for his shirt, flicking those buttons free with an ease borne of urgency. She was working her way down when he pulled her shirt wide and sank back, imprisoning her legs with his weight.

His eyes glinted like starlight, and he had the stark look of a man about to lose control, his flesh pulled tight over bone.

In one quick, ripping movement he tore his shirt free of his trousers and shrugged it off, leaving her in possession of a view that blew her mind.

She'd felt the solid muscle beneath his shirt, seen the way his wide shoulders and broad chest tapered down towards a narrow waist. But the naked reality stunned her.

Safiyah's throat dried. Karim was built like an ancient sculpture of idealised male athleticism. Dark skin and a dusting of even darker hair covered a muscled torso that drew her like iron to a magnet. Her hands lifted, pale against his bronzed flesh, to settle, fingers splayed, across satiny heat. Intrigued, she let them rove higher, over pectorals weighted with muscle and fuzz that tickled her palm.

Karim's ribs expanded into her palms as he snatched in air. In the soft darkness all she could hear was ragged breathing and the pulse of her blood, louder even than the shush of the waves.

Safiyah let her hands slide down across all that searing heat. She reached his belt, her knuckles grazing his flat belly and the tiny line of hair that disappeared into his trousers. Muscles tautened at the brush of her fingers, the tiny movement incredibly erotic.

'You want me.'

It wasn't a question. How could it be when he could read the need in her touch, in her quickened breathing, in the way she ate him up with her gaze? Yet she felt compelled to reply as he waited for the admission.

He'd challenged her to admit what she'd tried to hide, even from herself.

She swallowed, feeling that, despite their wedding vows last week, this was the real moment of truth between them. The moment of consent. With no witnesses but the vast sea and impervious stars. Where even in the shadows she could no longer hide.

'I want you, Karim.' She watched the quick rise of his chest on another mighty breath as if her words brought relief from pent-up pain. 'And you want me, don't you?'

His teeth gleamed in a smile that looked more like an expression of pain than pleasure.

'Of course.'

He took her hand and dragged it low, pressing it to his trousers. Her hand firmed on his erection and his eyelids lowered, his breath hissing as he pushed forward into her palm, his hand still cupping hers around him.

Heat suffused Safiyah. The sight of Karim half naked, questing after her touch with his head arched back in pleasure, was the most arousing thing she'd ever seen. The pulse between her legs quickened and she squirmed against his solid thighs. The sensations were simultaneously delicious and terrible. She'd wanted him for so long, even as she'd told herself she didn't.

The depth of her desire frightened her with its unfamiliarity. And that gave her the strength to drag her hand away.

Karim made as if to grab her hand, then stopped.

'You didn't come to me.' Her voice was a harsh rasp of fury and hurt as she struggled for breath. 'Ten. Whole. Days. You ignored me.'

How could she be sure he wasn't still playing some cruel game? Making her want, despite her better judgement?

Karim shook his head like a swimmer surfacing, trying to clear water from his eyes. 'You hold that against me?'

Suddenly Safiyah knew this was a bad idea. She lay half naked with a man who'd toyed with her before. Yet here she was, baring if not her soul her desires.

She tried to shift him, but those strong horseman's thighs held her in place.

'I'm sorry.'

Karim's apology froze her in place. Or maybe it was the way he trailed his index finger from her navel over her ribs till he reached her bra. Her nipples pebbled and she couldn't prevent the arch of her back, thrusting her breasts higher. He pressed his thumbs against her nipples and Safiyah gasped as pleasure shot straight to her core.

'I wanted to be with you,' he murmured, his voice low as he bent over her, his breath hot on the bare upper slopes of her breasts. 'But I couldn't. There was too much work to ensure key people were loyal to me, not Shakroun.'

He squeezed her breasts through the lacy bra and everything inside her turned molten.

'I worked day and night to make sure he couldn't mount a challenge.'

His words blurred under the force of her restless hunger but still he spoke.

'To ensure you and Tarek were safe.'

A mighty tremor racked Safiyah from head to toe. Whether from the idea of Karim—of anyone—putting her and her son first, or from the erotic intensity of his touch, she didn't know. But her indignation bled out like water through sand.

Karim reached behind her. Then her bra was undone and he pushed it high. She felt his thighs tighten around her hips. He bent, one hand closing around her bare breast while his mouth locked onto the other. No feather-light caress this time. Karim drew her nipple hard into his mouth and fire shot from her breast to her womb, spilling liquid sparks in a torrent through her blood. His hand kneaded her other breast and she bucked against his constraining legs, trying to shuffle her own legs wider.

Safiyah had never known such urgency, such need. Doubt was forgotten as her fingers dug like talons into his hips. She wanted him to move so she could spread her legs, wanted him to stay where he was and ease the hollow feeling inside her.

He moved, lifting his head and his hand from her body, and Safiyah bit back a cry of loss. Everything in her throbbed, aching for more. She'd felt a weak shadow of something like this in the past, but never so intense.

She was still absorbing that when Karim tugged her boots and socks off, tossing them aside. Then his hands were on the zip of her trousers, wrenching it undone and hauling the fabric down.

Safiyah lifted her hips, helping him drag her trousers and underwear down over her thighs, past her knees, then off. Cool air brushed her skin as she wrestled off her shirt and bra.

But when she'd finished, eager to help Karim undress, he hadn't started. Instead he knelt above her, his gaze like hot treacle, sliding over her bare body.

'You're beautiful.' His voice was hoarse, his hands possessive as they skimmed her trembling flesh.

Safiyah caught his wrists, holding them still as she met his eyes. 'You're slow. Take your clothes off.'

Never had she spoken so. Never had she made sexual demands. But something had altered within her.

Maybe it was that uninhibited race down the beach, unleashing a woman more elemental, less cautious than the one she'd learned to be. Maybe it was the fact that with Karim, for this moment at least, she felt able to admit to desire rather than just submit to another's wishes.

She felt strong as never before, even while his stance, as he loomed over her, was a reminder of his greater physical strength.

Karim laughed, the sound ripe and rich. Then he shifted off her. But instead of stripping his trousers off he moved lower, his hands spreading her bare legs. 'I like a woman who knows her mind.'

Then, before her stunned eyes, he sank onto the sand, his hands on her upper thighs, his dark head between her legs.

Safiyah felt a slow, slick caress that trailed fire. And then another caress, in a way no one had ever touched her before, and she shuddered, a deep groan lifting up from the base of her ribs to lock in her throat.

She shook all over, torn between shocked rejection and utter delight. Her hands locked in that dark hair, clawed at his scalp. She was going to push him away, because what he was doing made her feel undone in a way she'd never known. It scared her and aroused her and demanded too much of her.

She was about to—

The third caress—slower, harder, more deliberate—turned into something new. Safiyah opened her mouth to demand he stop when something slammed into her and she lost her voice, herself, lost everything in a searing, sparking, exquisitely perfect moment of rapture.

Not a moment but an eternity. It went on and on, rolling through her taut, trembling, burning body. It went beyond acute delight to a soul-deep conflagration that catapulted her into the stars.

Karim gathered her close in his arms as she shuddered and gasped and clung. He'd expected passion, known there'd be pleasure, but this...

He stopped trying to catalogue why this was different and merely held her. Finally Safiyah softened in his embrace and turned into him, nuzzling at his collarbone.

He was smiling in anticipation of entering that satisfaction-softened body when he registered wetness on his skin. He pulled back just enough to look down at her face. She watched him with stunned eyes. Silvery streaks tracked her cheeks.

He frowned. 'Safiyah? You're crying.' He'd had the occasional emotional lover, but the sight of Safiyah weeping unknotted something in his belly.

'Am I?' She raised a hand and wiped her cheeks. 'I'm

sorry. I just never—' She bit her bottom lip, as if to stop the words tumbling out.

'You never what?'

He waited, but her gaze slid away. He fancied he saw a blush rise in her cheeks, except surely in this light that was impossible. As was the notion her words had planted in his brain. It couldn't be. Could it…?

'Are you saying you've never had an orgasm?'

His voice rose in disbelief and he saw her face shutter. As if he'd accused her of something bad. It confounded him.

'Safiyah, talk to me.'

Five minutes ago it hadn't been conversation he'd wanted. As it was, his groin felt so hard he feared one wrong move might make him spill before he even got his trousers off. Yet he needed answers.

'It's nothing.'

Her mouth curved up in a smile that didn't fit.

Quickly she reached for his belt, starting to unbuckle it. 'I know what you want.'

Yet she didn't sound eager any more. She sounded… dutiful.

Incredibly, Karim felt his hand close on hers, stopping her when she would have pulled the belt undone. She was shaking, fine tremors rippling beneath the skin. The aftermath of her climax or something else?

'What I want is an answer.'

His voice emerged harsh. He felt her flinch and guilt eddied. Curiosity, too, about her relationship with Abbas. For years he hadn't let himself dwell on that. Now he was consumed by the need to know.

'But you haven't even—'

'I can wait.' He couldn't believe he was saying this when desire still rode him so painfully. 'Tell me, Safiyah.'

'It's nothing. I'm just a little…overwhelmed.'

'Because you've never climaxed before?'

The idea battered at him, making it difficult to think. It didn't change anything. So what if Safiyah hadn't found sexual satisfaction with her husband? So what if her eagerness to satisfy him suggested her experience had been about giving rather than receiving pleasure?

But it did matter.

Karim didn't understand why, but it did. He gathered her in and held her close till the last tremors subsided, even though it was torture in his aroused state. When she was warm and pliant in his arms he released her and moved away.

'Where are you going?'

She sounded shocked. As shocked as he felt.

'To get your clothes. We're going back to the palace.' He grimaced, his gait stiff and uncomfortable with his erection.

'Don't you want me?'

Her voice was a whisper, and when he turned she was sitting with her arms wrapped around her knees. Her pale flesh glimmered seductively and it took everything he had not to drop to his knees and continue what they'd begun.

'Of course I want you.' He drew a deep breath, strengthening his resolve. 'But when I take you, Safiyah, I want the first time to be in a comfortable bed—not hot and hard in the sand and over in two seconds.'

Which sounded good in theory, yet Karim wasn't sure how he was going to make it last—bed or no bed.

Why, precisely, the location suddenly mattered, he wasn't sure. Except he suspected Safiyah hadn't been an equal partner in sex before.

Karim didn't want her sharing his bed out of duty. He wanted her as she'd been moments before, full of passion and delight. She deserved more than a quick coupling on the beach.

He wanted to make their first time together special.

Karim refused to dwell on what that meant.

CHAPTER NINE

SAFIYAH LISTENED TO the sound of the shower in the next room and slumped down to sit on the end of the bed. Karim had spoken barely a word on the ride back to the summer palace, or after they'd left the stables for their bedroom.

Their bedroom.

Instead of horrifying her, those words settled in her mind like a comforting blanket. Because she'd given up hiding from the truth. She wanted her new husband and she looked forward to being with him. Even though she knew from previous experience that the actual sex act would be less than satisfying, she still wanted him.

Because he'd been the first man to give her an orgasm?

Her lips curved at the memory.

That would be an easy explanation. But Safiyah refused to settle for anything less than the truth.

She'd never stopped wanting Karim, even after he'd treated her so callously.

Throughout her first marriage she'd compartmentalised, putting her feelings for Karim away in a box marked 'Ancient History', devoting herself to her husband. But now there was nothing holding back those old feelings and they were stronger than ever.

She shifted, trying to ease the ache between her legs—so inexplicable given that stunning climax. Beneath her clothes she felt the abrasive scratch of sand. What she wanted—apart from Karim—was a wash, but he'd stalked straight to the bathroom and she, out of training and habit, was content to wait on her husband's wishes.

Except Safiyah *wasn't* content. She felt edgy and uncomfortable. She wanted a wash and she wanted Karim.

His words kept replaying in her head. He wanted her in a comfortable bed where he could take his time. He didn't want sex to be hot and hard and over in two seconds.

She knew about sex that was over almost before it had begun, and she was accustomed to the listless sense that she'd missed out on something just beyond her reach. Now she knew what she'd missed and she wanted more. How would it feel to reach that pinnacle of bliss with Karim moving inside her?

Safiyah shivered and wrapped her arms around herself, trying to hold in the breathless excitement. An image rose in her head of herself following Karim into the bathroom, stripping off her crumpled sticky clothes and joining him in the shower. Her skin drew tight and her palms dampened as she remembered how good he looked without his shirt.

How would he look totally naked?

Once more she shifted. But nothing could ease that restless ache. Except Karim.

Abbas would have been horrified at her making a sexual advance. He'd always taken the initiative. Not that she'd ever wanted to.

But then he'd never caressed her with his mouth the way Karim had. Never made her fly in ecstasy and never, for that matter, pulled back without taking his own pleasure. Seeing Karim do that tonight had stunned her, making her question what she knew about him.

For years she'd believed him callous, even cruel. Yet he'd adopted her son, made Tarek his heir. There'd been acts of kindness enough to make her think this forced marriage wouldn't be all bad.

Safiyah thought of Karim's very obvious erection as he'd gathered the horses and helped her up, of his grimace as he'd mounted and turned his horse towards the palace. She thought of his ebony head buried in the V between her thighs and the extraordinary experience he'd bestowed upon her.

Karim was a conundrum. But one thing was obvious— he didn't follow Abbas's rules. Whatever rules they followed in this marriage were for her and Karim to decide.

The realisation made her feel suddenly strong.

Toeing off her shoes, Safiyah rose and marched, heart hammering, to the bathroom door. She opened it and slipped in. There was no steam to obscure her husband's naked body. He stood, palms flat on the tiled wall, head bowed beneath the sluicing water that trailed down over wide shoulders and a tapering body to firm, round buttocks and long, muscled legs.

Ignoring the doubts pecking at her determination, Safiyah stripped off her clothes, shivering as the fabric scraped across her hyper-aware flesh. Nervousness almost stopped her, but determination won out. She padded across to the shower, opened the glass door and stepped in.

An arctic chill enveloped her and she yelped as the water sprayed her.

'Safiyah?'

Stunned eyes met hers as she recoiled from the cold water. But when she tried to retreat she found her way barred by one long arm. The other reached for the taps. Seconds later the water turned warm.

'What are you doing here?'

'What are *you* doing standing under cold water?'

One black eyebrow crooked. 'Why do men usually take cold showers?'

Involuntarily she looked down. The cold water had done

its job. He was no longer rampantly erect. But, she realised with a rush of heat, Karim still looked well endowed.

The restless feeling between her legs intensified and she shifted her weight—only to brush up against that brawny arm stretched between her and the exit, reminding her abruptly of her own nakedness.

Her brows knitted. She didn't understand him. 'You don't want sex, then?'

Her stomach plunged. It was like when they'd courted. She'd believed then that Karim cared for her, might even love her. She'd daily expected him to propose. Instead, when she and her father had been called away because Rana had needed them desperately, Karim hadn't even bothered to say goodbye. She'd gone from happiness and breathless expectation to disbelief and hurt in the blink of an eye.

Safiyah reached for the door.

This time he didn't just bar her way—he took her shoulders and turned her to face him. 'Of course I want you. Didn't I tell you so?'

Her heart gave a little shimmy when he said he wanted *her*, not merely sex. Oh, she had it bad. But she couldn't find the energy to worry about that now.

His gaze dropped to her bare breasts and Safiyah saw the spark of masculine appreciation in that look. A pulse ticked at his temple and suddenly she *felt* his stare. His eyes met hers and her breath snagged. Such intensity, all focused on her.

'Then why don't you do something about it?'

His laugh was like a crack of thunder, sharp and short. 'Because I want to make it good for you, not explode the minute I touch you.'

That was the second time he'd said that. She couldn't decide if she felt flattered or frustrated.

'You've already made it good for me.'

Better than she'd ever experienced, though she didn't

say that. It was bad enough that he'd guessed her relative inexperience. She refused to act as if this was a big deal.

Safiyah reached for him, her eyes rounding as she discovered him already growing hard.

Karim's smile was a tight twist of the lips, then he leaned in and whispered, 'There's more to come.'

But instead of turning off the water and opening the shower door Karim crowded her back against the tiled wall. He was all heat and slick muscle and she trembled at the feel of skin sliding against skin, heat against heat. Excitement spiked a fizz of effervescence in her blood.

The flesh in her hand was heavy now, soft skin over rearing steel, his erection larger than she'd expected.

As if reading the scurry of sudden anxiety along her spine Karim stilled, then pulled back so he was no longer pinning her to the wall. 'We'll go back to the bedroom and take things slow.'

He reached out an arm to switch off the taps, but Safiyah wrapped her fingers around his wrist. 'No.' Those remarkable eyes met hers, ripe with question. 'I don't want to wait.'

To reinforce her words she pulled one of his hands towards her, planting it over her breast. Instantly his fingers moulded to her with exquisite pressure and the flesh in her hand swelled as Karim stepped closer and his erection slid against her.

Safiyah bit her cheek against the sudden wash of delight. 'Don't.'

Karim's other hand brushed her cheek, her mouth, pressing her bottom lip till she opened her mouth and tasted him with her tongue.

'Witch!'

Those green eyes seemed to eat her up. A hairy thigh, solid with muscle, insinuated itself between her legs. And a moment later she felt his touch in that most intimate place.

Safiyah's gaze clung to his as he deftly stroked her, evoking a response that made her hand tighten around him.

'You like that, don't you, Safiyah? And you liked it when I kissed you there too. Didn't you?'

She swallowed, trying to find her voice and failing. Instead she nodded, wondering how much longer she could stay on her feet when each deliberate slide of his fingers made her feel weak and trembling.

She loved what he was doing but she didn't want to be weak. She wanted to participate. So she took him in both hands, cupping and stroking, delighted when his eyelids lowered, turning his eyes to gleaming slits.

His nostrils flared and his strong features looked stark and tight. He groaned. 'So much for taking it slow.' Swiftly he moved her hands away, placing them on his shoulders and then lifting her up off the floor. 'Hook your legs over my hips.'

The words emerged as a terse order, but Safiyah read his juddering pulse and the convulsive movement of his throat as he swallowed. Karim was at the edge of his control, just as she'd been on the beach. The thought thrilled her and she complied, wrapping herself around those tight hips, clinging to his wide shoulders.

But there was no time for triumph. Instead she bit back a gasp as he brought them together in one slow, deliberate thrust.

Safiyah's eyes were snared on his and she couldn't look away. She fancied she saw his darken as a second thrust unlocked something deep within her and sensations rushed through her. This felt unfamiliar and a little scary—especially as she was pinned high against his tall frame, not even supporting herself. Yet at the same time she exulted in it when she moved to meet him and felt a shudder rip through him.

'Yes,' he whispered through gritted teeth. 'Like that.'

His big hands held her hips, helping her angle herself to meet him. Instead of feeling used, Safiyah felt powerful. She'd chosen this. Nor was it solely about Karim's pleasure. She craved this with every cell in her body. And, impossibly, the flames she'd felt on the beach were flickering again deep inside her.

Those flames skyrocketed when Karim palmed her belly and pressed his thumb down on that sensitive bud between her legs. Safiyah jerked as lightning sheared through her.

Karim grinned, the picture of male smugness.

She responded by tightening her muscles around him.

His grin solidified and his powerful thrusts turned jerky.

Safiyah saw the bunch of his muscles, the tendons standing proud in his neck and his eyes glazing.

But this wasn't a contest. Nor was it duty. This was what she'd craved for so long. This was Karim and her together, connected in a way that felt almost too profound to be just sex.

Then all thinking stopped as Karim changed the angle of his thrusts. For a moment everything stilled. A second later she was flung into a cataclysm that melded delight and something much more far-reaching.

Safiyah heard a deep shout, felt the hard pump within her and fell into ecstasy, holding Karim tight as he gathered her in.

They lay sprawled sideways across the bed. The pillows had long since disappeared, but no matter. Karim felt as if it would take a tsunami to make him move.

He lay on his back, his bones melting into the mattress, his body limp with satiation. With a supreme effort he slid his hand through the spill of Safiyah's hair, lying like a silken cloud across his chest and shoulder. Predictably, even that simple caress stirred an eagerness for more.

She lay draped over him—a lush, erotic blanket. If he'd

had more energy he'd have devoted himself to exploring that delectable body again. He'd been fascinated by her reactions, a mix of wholehearted responsiveness and shyness. But after a night devoted to carnal pleasure, giving in again and again to the urge for just one more taste of his bride, he'd have to wait to summon some strength.

That didn't stop his mind from working. On the contrary, it was busier than ever, trying to make sense of tonight's events with something that in another man might have come close to panic.

But Karim never panicked. He assessed, reviewed, and determined the logical course of action. It was what he'd been trained to do.

Right now logic wasn't helping.

Sex with Safiyah was phenomenal. Urgent and explosive, yet deeply satisfying. Terribly addictive. The more they shared, the more they wanted.

Karim had been taken aback by the demands of his libido, as if after years of denial he was making up for lost time. As if sex with Safiyah was more real, more satisfying, than with any other lover. Even when they did no more than lie together, body to body, sharing the occasional gentle caress, it felt *different* from previous experiences.

The notion was unsettling. Karim had expected their first night together to be memorable. He'd waited long enough for it, having never quite managed to excise her from his memory. But this was so much more than he'd anticipated.

He thought back over his actions.

The way he'd denied himself instant gratification on the beach because he'd decided on a whim that their first time needed to be memorable. It had been memorable, all right. Harder and hotter and more intense than anything he could recall, with Safiyah's lush breasts jouncing up and down against him, her welcoming body wrapped so tight around him he'd detonated with the force of a rocket.

The way he'd spent so much time denying his own pleasure in order to bring her to climax again and again, despite her pleas and her pouting demands that he take her fully. And his desperation whenever he'd relented and joined her.

He'd taken his fill but he'd done far more. It was as if he'd tried to imprint himself on her consciousness, to make her associate ecstasy with him and only him. As if he'd wanted to obliterate any memory of her first husband.

Was he jealous of a dead man?

Of course not—especially since he'd learned that Abbas hadn't had the sense or generosity to please his wife in bed. The idea of him using Safiyah for his own satisfaction but giving none in return twisted like a drill boring through Karim's gut. He hadn't liked the man but now he despised him.

Yet that didn't explain the other riddle. Why it was that with Safiyah sex seemed more than just an expression of lust and physical pleasure.

He frowned into the darkness, telling himself there was a reasonable explanation. Release after the stress of recent weeks, perhaps?

Safiyah shifted as if to roll away and he stopped her. 'Stay.'

'You're awake?'

'Barely.'

She chuckled, the sound rich and appealing, but it was the way he felt the vibration of her laugh through his body, his hunger to hear more, that threatened to undo him.

Why, he didn't know. Except suddenly there came the certainty that this sense of closeness, of emotional intimacy, was dangerous.

Through the night physical desire had been transformed into the illusion of something more profound. Something akin to what he'd felt when he'd first known Safiyah. When she'd had the power to hurt him—and not just his pride, he finally admitted, but something buried even deeper.

That wouldn't do. No matter how spectacular the sex, Karim needed to remember who he'd married and why. He couldn't allow himself to be lured into thinking this was more than sexual attraction.

'Tell me about Abbas.'

Safiyah stiffened and he heard her indrawn breath. Then she rolled away to lie on her back. Though he'd decided to establish some distance, Karim had to make a conscious effort not to haul her back into his arms.

'Why?'

'Why not?' He turned towards her, pillowing his head on one bent arm.

'You really want to do this *now*?'

He couldn't read her features but the discordant note in her voice sounded defensive.

'Your first marriage is hardly a secret.' He kept his voice even, though it still rankled that she'd gone straight from him to Abbas.

That last night, when she and her father had stayed at the Za'daqi palace, she'd agreed to meet Karim secretly. She'd been his for the taking, though no marriage contract had been drawn up.

Except Ashraf had found him in the secluded garden instead, breaking the news of the medical results that had proved he wasn't the Sheikh's son.

The shocking revelation had pushed everything, even Safiyah, from Karim's head. It hadn't been till later that he'd realised she must have come to their rendezvous and overheard their conversation. After learning he was illegitimate, she'd dumped him for Abbas.

Now she scrabbled for a sheet, dragging it up to cover

herself. 'There's nothing much to tell.' Her voice was brisk. 'He wanted to marry into my clan.'

'Go on.' Was it masochism that made him want to hear more?

'Rana, my sister, caught his eye first. She was studying in the capital and she was…is…intelligent and pretty.'

Her words struck Karim. It sounded almost as if Safiyah believed her sister outshone her.

'But then she got sick. Marriage wasn't possible. And so—'

'And so you jumped at the chance to marry a king?'

For a second she didn't answer. Then, tucking the sheet close around her, she rolled to face him. They were less than an arm's length apart, yet it seemed like more. Even in the darkness he felt the chill in her stare.

'When I was in Za'daq you weren't the only one whose father was unwell. My father had received a terminal diagnosis, though he didn't tell me straight away. He knew he'd be dead within months.'

Karim frowned. He'd never have guessed. Safiyah's father had looked so hale and hearty.

'He was old-fashioned in some ways, and desperate to get Rana and me "safely settled", as he called it, before he died. When Rana got sick…' another pause, '…all his hopes rested on me. He wanted me to marry well—not just for myself, but so Rana would be cared for while she recovered.'

Karim thought of the woman he'd met during the wedding. If she'd been seriously ill it didn't show now.

'So it was all your father's doing?'

On learning of Karim's illegitimacy her father would have pushed her towards another man. But if Safiyah had loved Karim she'd have stuck with him. She wouldn't have let herself be driven into another man's bed. The fact she'd done just that still stuck in his gullet.

'My father suggested it. Abbas agreed and I…consented.'

Karim cursed the darkness that prevented him reading Safiyah. Something in her voice intrigued him. Despite his residual anger he felt reluctant admiration that she'd admitted it had been her choice.

He breathed deep. Time to let this rest. Yet…

'It was a happy marriage?'

Safiyah scanned the dark form before her, trying and failing to read his expression.

A happy marriage?

She almost laughed. She'd believed once that she'd have just that—with Karim, of all people. The absurdity of those dreams tasted like ash on her tongue.

She'd been all but forced into marriage. Technically, she could have said no. But with her father fading before her eyes and both of them worried about Rana, Abbas's offer had been a *fait accompli*. Karim had turned his back on her. Her father's health had been spiralling down as worry increased and they'd struggled to find the care Rana needed after her breakdown.

Abbas had taken care of everything. He'd got Rana immediate entry to an exclusive clinic renowned for its excellence. A clinic which usually had a long waiting list. Safiyah had been so grateful, and in the circumstances what reason could she have given for rejecting him?

'It was a good marriage,' she said finally.

If by *good* she meant that it had conformed to expectations.

Publicly, Abbas had honoured her. Yet otherwise he'd had little to do with her except when he'd wanted sex or needed a hostess. He'd helped her support her sister, and in his own way had been pleased with his son—if disturbingly distant. And if he had been too autocratic for her taste and hadn't loved her—well, he'd been the King and she'd never expected love. She'd done her best to play her royal role.

'A good marriage? Not a happy one?' Karim leaned close, as if intent on her answer.

Safiyah stiffened. Despite the joy Karim had brought her tonight, she didn't have the emotional resources to deal with an autopsy on her first marriage. She'd survived it and that was what mattered. Dredging up the details would only reinforce the fact that, despite tonight's sexual satisfaction, she'd given herself in another loveless marriage.

She swallowed hard, forcing down the metallic taste of despair. Could she really go through this again? Especially when this was a hundred times worse because part of her kept hoping for some sign that Karim cared for her. Even though she *knew* that was impossible.

'That's enough, Karim. I don't ask you about your past. I don't delve into your secrets.'

In the gloom she saw him stiffen as if she'd struck him. Because she'd answered back or because he had secrets he wouldn't share? She was too weary and upset to ask.

'You'll have to forgive my curiosity.' But his voice held no apology. Instead it cut like honed steel. 'I thought it would be useful to know more about you since we've undertaken to spend our lives together.'

He sounded anything but thrilled about that! He made it sound like a prison sentence.

Gone was the passionate lover. Gone the tenderness that had wound itself around her foolish, unthinking heart and made her begin to believe that miracles might be possible.

Karim's haughty tone reminded her exactly why they'd married.

Pragmatism, not love.

Never love.

Safiyah choked back the sob that thickened her voice. Perhaps she was vulnerable after tonight's unprecedented experiences, but suddenly the idea of spending her whole future in a marriage where she'd have to pretend not to crave what she could never have was too much.

'Don't bother about that,' she said. 'A successful royal marriage doesn't require you to know me or I you. In fact, it will work best if we meet as polite strangers.'

She gathered the sheet tight around her and rolled away. 'I'm going to sleep now. I've got a headache.'

CHAPTER TEN

POLITE STRANGERS.

Karim grimaced. The idea was ludicrous, but that was exactly what they were. Even after seven nights away from the capital on their supposed honeymoon.

He swore and shoved his chair back from the desk, swamped by the discontent that hounded him whenever he tried and failed to break through Safiyah's reserve.

Or when he tried to determine why doing that was so important to him.

Every morning and for a couple of hours in the evening Karim worked, grappling with the multitude of matters requiring the new Sheikh's attention. Each day he breakfasted with Tarek and Safiyah, and they spent the afternoons together as a family. For Karim was determined to establish a good relationship with his new son. Not for Tarek a life in which the only male role model was a man he hated spending time with.

To Karim's surprise the boy had accepted him. Not only that but, given the chance, Tarek dogged Karim's footsteps as if fascinated by him.

Or just previously starved of male attention?

The picture Karim had built of Abbas was of a man with little time for his wife or son. A man caught up in the business of ruling, or perhaps a man too wrapped up in himself to care about anyone else.

That possibility stirred indignation in Karim's breast.

His own dysfunctional family had made him impatient with those who didn't appreciate the value of what they had. Which was why he was determined to make this work— for all of them.

Yet between Karim and Safiyah there yawned a void. Safiyah held herself aloof. Each day it was like conversing at a formal banquet with a foreign ambassador—all charm on the surface but with neither letting their guard down.

He'd never met a woman so adept at avoiding discussions about herself. Whenever he pressed for more she lifted her eyebrows as if surprised and deftly changed the subject.

If she'd fobbed him off with trivialities it wouldn't have worked, but Safiyah was a fount of knowledge on Assaran politics. Her shrewd observations on key individuals, on brewing issues and provincial power-plays were informative and incredibly useful to a man shouldering the burden of ruling a new country.

The only time she let her guard slip was in bed. Or in the shower. Or during their midnight swims. Or wherever else they had sex. Then she was a siren who drove him wild with her responsiveness and, increasingly, her demands.

Sometimes he felt as if he was really connecting to the vibrant woman hiding behind the mask of conformable queen and wife. He glimpsed something in her velvety eyes that hinted she was there—the woman he'd once believed her to be. But then, after sex, the barriers came up like steel barricades. Shutting him out.

Karim wasn't emotionally needy. He hadn't been since he was a child and his mother had abandoned him to the mercy of a tyrant. He'd made himself self-sufficient in every way. So it wasn't for his own sake that he wanted to break down the wall between him and Safiyah. It was so they could create a sound footing for a future together, to bring up Tarek and any future children.

His groin tightened and his pulse skipped faster at the idea of fathering Safiyah's children. He'd been semi-aroused all morning, despite the hours dealing with budget papers and plans for law reform. The sea breeze through the window reminded him of their race down the beach that first night here—that fever of need as he'd stripped Safiyah and given her a first taste of rapture.

Karim closed his eyes as a shudder ran through him. Hunger and longing. And regret. Because after the triumphant sex and that incredible sense of closeness she'd said coldly that it was best if they were strangers.

It was what he'd visualised when he'd first imagined this marriage. Keeping her at a distance, using her to secure his standing in this new country and for personal pleasure—not least the satisfaction of having at his mercy the woman who'd spurned him.

But from the start he'd wanted more.

Frowning, Karim shut down his computer and stood, rolling his shoulders.

He'd erred in pushing her for details about Abbas that night in bed. They'd both been exhausted after a sexual marathon that had left them off balance. Yet Karim had been driven by an urgency to establish control over circumstances that had suddenly seemed more complex and fraught than he'd anticipated.

He'd expected great sex, given the constant shimmer of attraction between them. Yet he hadn't expected to *feel* so much when he finally bedded Safiyah. It had been as if the years had peeled away and he still believed she was the one woman for him. As if her happiness was important to him.

His glance strayed to the brilliant blue sky outside the window. It was their last afternoon at the small summer palace. His plans for today would surely help him break down Safiyah's defences.

* * *

'A picnic lunch?'

Safiyah met Karim's glinting eyes. His brows slanted up at her surprise, giving him a saturnine appearance that was both goading and sexy.

It was appalling the way such a little thing made her knees weaken and her insides liquefy. At breakfast today she'd been reduced to wordless yearning just by the crook of Karim's mouth in the hint of a smile.

That half-smile had reminded her of last night, when Karim had teased her mercilessly with his mouth and hands till she'd begged for him to take her. Last night there'd been something in his expression, too. Something she couldn't name and didn't want to, for she feared she'd make a fool of herself, imagining tender emotions when he had none.

She was his convenient bride. Nothing more.

'Yes, a picnic. It's all arranged.'

He made it sound like a typical royal event, with retainers on hand to serve them. She didn't particularly enjoy formality, but if it meant less time alone with Karim that was a good thing. Because it got harder by the day not to be seduced by his charm.

'I'm sure Tarek will like that.'

'Oh, I know he will.'

Was Karim laughing at her? That gleam in those dark eyes—

'He was thrilled when I told him. Ah, here he is.'

Safiyah turned to see Tarek running from his room, not in his usual shorts and T-shirt, but in the trousers and boots he wore for visiting the stables.

'Mama, Mama, we have a surprise for you.'

He stopped beside Karim and looked up at the tall man. Then, to Safiyah's surprise, her son lifted his small hand and Karim's long fingers enfolded it.

A pang pierced her lungs. Could she be jealous of the burgeoning closeness between the two? That would make her pathetic. It was good for Tarek that Karim made time for him and seemed to enjoy his company. Her son had bloomed since coming here, becoming more and more the carefree little boy she'd seen in snatches since Abbas's repressive influence had gone.

'A surprise? How lovely.'

Her boy nodded gravely, then frowned. 'But you need other shoes. For safety.'

He looked up to Karim, who nodded. 'That's right. We don't wear sandals around horses.'

'Horses?'

That explained Tarek's beaming smile. So they were having a picnic in the stables? Despite her attempts to distance herself a little from Karim, she couldn't help smiling at the idea. Tarek was fascinated by horses and she'd promised to teach him to ride.

'That sounds like fun. I'll be right back.'

But when she went to the stables there was no picnic laid out. Instead she found Tarek, grinning from ear to ear, wearing a riding helmet and mounted astride a tubby little pony almost as wide as it was high.

'Surprise!' He threw out his arms, bouncing in the saddle so Karim, holding the pony's leading rope, put out a hand to steady him.

'Easy, Tarek. What have I said about sitting still and not frightening Amin?'

The pony didn't look perturbed—merely shook its head and stood patiently.

Safiyah stopped in her tracks, torn between shock and delight. Tarek looked so enthusiastic, his smile like a beacon. She grinned back at him. He really was coming out of the shell of reserve that had so worried her.

But at the same time she forced down a sliver of something less positive—the feeling that she'd been excluded. *She'd* wanted to teach Tarek to ride, had looked forward to it.

Yet she couldn't be selfish enough to begrudge him his excitement. This was a positive change from Abbas, who'd never made time to be with Tarek, much less encouraged him to learn anything other than court etiquette.

'You're riding? Karim has been teaching you?'

Maybe that explained Tarek's recent willingness to have a nap in the afternoon. Before coming here he'd been adamant he no longer needed a rest. Had he and Karim secretly spent nap time in the stables?

Tarek nodded. 'Brushing Amin and feeding him and learning how to sit.' He chewed his lip. 'But not really *riding...*' He looked up wistfully at Karim.

Karim's eyes met hers. 'We thought you'd like to teach him that.'

His voice was suede brushing across her skin and Safiyah shivered in response.

'You're the expert rider in the family. I've told Tarek how you used to compete.'

Silly how much his words affected her. She drank them in like desert earth sucking in life-giving water. Because it was so long since she'd received praise? Or because it was for something she'd once excelled at?

But even after years of being denied access to the animals she loved she wasn't that needy. This warm feeling came from the way Tarek and Karim looked at her. Tarek with excitement and admiration and Karim with...

Safiyah wrenched her gaze away. Karim was doing what he'd promised—building a bond with Tarek, creating a sense of family so her boy could thrive. So they could present the image of a solid family unit. Karim was pragmatic, that was all. It would be crazy to read more into his actions.

She focused on Tarek. 'You're sitting up nice and straight. I'm impressed. Are you ready to ride out?'

'Can I? Can I really?' He jumped up and down in the saddle, then almost immediately subsided, leaning forward to pat the pony reassuringly. 'Sorry, Amin. I didn't mean to scare you.'

The pony flicked its ear at the sound of his name but otherwise didn't budge.

Safiyah suppressed a smile. 'You found a very calm pony, Karim. I only hope he moves as well as he stands.'

Karim passed her the leading rope. 'Time to find out.'

Amin did, indeed, move. In fact he turned out to be an ideal learner's mount—placid, but not obstinate, content to circle the courtyard again and again while Tarek learned the basics.

'I had no idea what you two were up to,' Safiyah said as they stopped before Karim. Despite her stern self-talk, she found herself smiling into those glinting eyes. 'You kept the secret well.'

He shrugged. 'We kept Amin at the far end of the stable, away from the other horses, so you wouldn't see him. He's only been here a couple of days. I don't think Tarek could have kept the secret any longer.'

Tarek piped up. 'I wanted to tell you, Mama, but I wanted to surprise you with how much I know.' He rattled off information about grooming his pony and even caring for his tack.

Safiyah raised her eyebrows.

'I told Tarek that if he had a pony he had to learn how to look after it.' Karim caught her eye.

'I agree.' She turned to her son. 'You've learned so much. I'm proud of you.'

He grinned. 'Can we go now? Can we?'

'Go?' Safiyah looked from Tarek to Karim.

'Our picnic, remember?' He turned and went into the

stable, emerging with her horse, already saddled. 'Up you get.' When Safiyah hesitated he continued. 'You and Tarek will ride. I'll lead the pony.'

Karim would walk, leaving her and Tarek to ride? She couldn't imagine many men of her acquaintance doing that—especially Abbas, even if he *had* been able to ride. Usually women and children tagged along while the man took precedence.

'Hurry up, Safiyah. I don't know about you, but I'm hungry.'

There was no impatience in Karim's expression, just a twinkle of amusement that she found far too attractive. With one last look at Tarek she took the reins and swung up into the saddle.

They didn't ride far, and not down to the beach—for which she was grateful. Even with Karim holding the leading rope, the track there was steep and would challenge a first-time rider. Instead they went to a sheltered grove a little way along the headland.

The view across the sea was spectacular, but what held Safiyah's eye was the tent erected for their convenience. It was tall enough to stand up in. The floor was covered with carpets and cushions. And she caught the glint of silver from platters, jugs and intricately decorated goblets. Cool boxes stood in one corner, no doubt packed with their picnic meal.

The place looked inviting and, she realised, deserted. The servants who'd set up this temporary camp had clearly returned to the palace. Maybe that accounted for the sense of intimacy here. There was silence but for the snort of the horses, Tarek's chatter and the whisper of the sea below.

She caught Karim's gaze on her. Warmth swarmed through her, climbing to her cheeks. Suddenly the tent with all its rich furnishings looked like the setting for seduction.

She remembered that morning, when Karim had persuaded her to stay in bed, ostensibly by reaching out one hand to stroke her bare body. But it had been the searing hunger in his expression that had held her there. For she'd been consumed by a matching hunger.

How dangerous it was, trying to keep her heart whole while sharing her husband's bed. This wasn't like her marriage to Abbas. Then there'd been no difficulty in maintaining an emotional distance. But with Karim—

'What are you thinking?'

His voice hit that baritone note that never failed to make Safiyah feel weak and wanton.

'I...' Her gaze shifted and she noticed for the first time that one end of the tent was a cosy bower, where a couple of Tarek's toys were propped against fluffy pillows. A kite lay beside them.

Safiyah swallowed, her throat closing convulsively as emotion see-sawed. This looked...felt...like the action of more than a man taking a pragmatic approach. It felt like the action of a man who cared.

'Safiyah?'

Suddenly he was before her, looking down from under sombre brows.

'What's wrong?'

She shook her head, swallowing the reckless words that crammed her mouth. Pushing away the almost overwhelming urge to pretend this was real. Once she'd yearned for love, had believed in it with all her heart. To her dismay it seemed even the hard lessons of the last years hadn't banished that craving.

'Mama! Karim! I'm starving. Aren't you?' Tarek raced into the tent, lifting the lid on one of the cool boxes.

'Nothing's wrong.' She aimed a vague smile in Karim's direction. 'You seem to have thought of everything. Thank you.'

Before he could question further, she hurried after her son. 'Wait, Tarek. You need to wash your hands first.'

Again Karim felt he'd missed his opportunity with Safiyah. In the rare moments when it seemed they were on the brink of something more than sex, or a purely dynastic marriage, the possibility shimmered for an instant and then shattered.

Was it weakness to want more?

He'd told himself he wanted to secure their future. If he and Safiyah knew and trusted each other they'd create a unit that would underpin his new role.

Or did his need for more from Safiyah have another explanation?

Personal experience made him particularly sympathetic to Tarek's situation. A childhood devoid of love had made Karim determined to do better for the boy than his own parents had done.

His mouth twisted in distaste. *His parents*. He didn't know who his father was. His mother had died when he was young and her lover had never lifted a finger to contact Karim.

Maybe that was it. Apart from Ashraf, Karim was alone. Maybe his determination to build a family unit wasn't just for Tarek's sake, but his own.

He scowled. The notion was absurd. He had a plan and he was determined to make it work. That was all. The throb of anticipation now, as he joined Safiyah and Tarek, simply meant he was pleased at his progress so far. No more than that.

Yet a couple of hours later Karim had ceased to think in terms of plans and progress. Relaxed and replete, he found himself enjoying Tarek's amusing chatter and Safiyah's company. Their easy conversation seemed the most natural thing in the world.

How long since he'd done something as simple and fine as enjoying a picnic?

The answer was easy. Never.

His early life had been filled with royal responsibilities. There'd been no lazy afternoons. And since he'd left Za'daq he'd thrown himself into his investment business, needing to fill the huge gap in his world where duty had once been.

Now he stood in the centre of the clearing, one hand on Tarek's shoulder as the boy leaned into him, his head flung back to watch the red kite bobbing above them.

'Look, Karim! Look, Mama! It's flying.'

'I'm looking, sweetie. It's wonderful.'

'Karim can teach you too.' The boy twisted to look up at Karim. 'Can't you?'

'Of course.'

The boy relinquished the kite's string and scampered across to his mother, dragging her back to Karim. 'Here.'

Ignoring Safiyah's rueful smile, Karim stepped closer. Immediately the light perfume of her skin teased him. So instead of merely handing the kite to her he moved behind her, wrapping his arm around her waist. He felt her sudden intake of breath and the silk of her hair against his mouth as he brought his hand to hers, offering her the kite.

For a moment she stood stiffly. Then the wind jerked the kite and she gave an exclamation of surprise and delight.

'Careful. Watch it doesn't dip too low,' he warned.

She tugged, and together they moved to catch the up-draught. It took some manoeuvring, and a near miss, but soon they had it flying high again.

'Thanks. I've never done this before. I didn't know it was so thrilling.'

She smiled up at him over her shoulder and the glow of her pleasure drenched him like sunlight banishing the night's shadows. Gone was the reserve she usually maintained when they weren't having sex.

Karim's chest expanded as pleasure filled him. 'I haven't either. That makes us all novices.'

'You haven't?' She looked astonished. 'I thought you must have learned as a boy.'

Karim shook his head. He was about to explain that there'd been little time for childish pursuits in the Za'daqi royal court when someone entered the clearing. His secretary—looking grim.

'Your Majesty… Madam.'

He bowed deep and Karim saw his shoulders rise as if he were catching his breath. Karim's smile froze. Such an interruption could only mean serious news.

'Sir, may we speak in private?'

Karim felt Safiyah tense and tightened his hold on her. 'You may speak in front of the Sheikha.'

This was more than some scheduling problem. With his staring eyes, the man looked to be in shock. Karim braced himself. *Not Ashraf. Not his brother…*

'Very well, Your Majesty.' He hesitated, then abruptly blurted out, 'There's a report in the media about your… background. Claiming that your father was—'

He stopped, and Karim came to his rescue. 'Not my father?' Weariness mingled with relief that there hadn't been a tragedy. But clearly there was no escaping some secrets.

'Yes, Your Majesty.' The man stepped forward and proffered a tablet.

Karim took it, reading swiftly. The news piece was carefully worded, but it noted that if Karim's father hadn't been the Sheikh of Zad'aq Karim had no claim to the title of Prince. The implication being that without that the Assaran Royal Council wouldn't have considered him a contender for its throne.

Regret surfaced that today's pleasure should be blighted by an old scandal that he'd thought dead and buried. But then Karim squared his shoulders and concentrated on what needed to be done.

* * *

Safiyah read the headline and froze. When Karim dropped his arm from her waist, moving away with his secretary, Safiyah took the tablet from him with numb fingers.

She felt blank inside…except for a creeping chill where Karim's body warmth had been.

'Mama! Look out!'

Safiyah's head jerked up. The line of the kite was slipping and she tightened her grip on it. With an effort she conjured a smile for Tarek, even as her mind whirled at the news story and Karim's matter-of-fact response to it.

It couldn't be true. The very idea was preposterous.

'Here.' She passed Tarek the kite. 'You can have it, but you must stay here where I can see you.'

A glance revealed Karim and his secretary deep in discussion. Karim was showing none of the outrage she'd have expected if the story were false. Her husband looked stern but calm.

Her husband.

But who was he if he wasn't the son of the Sheikh of Za'daq?

It felt as if the ground beneath her feet had buckled.

Slowly she moved into the shade of one of the trees fringing the clearing. Intent on answers, yet excluded from the terse conversation going on metres away, she turned back to the article. Reaching the end, she went back to the beginning and read it again, astounded.

It was an outrageous allegation, and no definitive proof was provided, though there was mention of a medical technician willing to swear to it. The story claimed Karim's mother had been unfaithful to her husband before deserting him and that the old Sheikh had only learned Karim wasn't his just before his death.

The report insinuated that Karim had then been banished by his younger half-brother, Ashraf, who'd threat-

ened to proclaim the truth if he didn't renounce his claim
to the Za'daqi throne. Yet when Safiyah had seen Karim
and Ashraf together at the coronation they'd seemed on the
best of terms. And Karim had been full of smiles for his
sister-in-law, Tori.

'Seen enough?'

Karim stood before her, eyes narrowed to gleaming slits,
hands clenched at his sides, in a wide stance that was pure
male challenge. Out of the corner of her eye she saw the
secretary hurry back towards the palace. Tarek scampered
around, ignoring them all, watching the kite.

'Is it true?' Her voice sounded unfamiliar.

Karim's mouth tightened, his jaw jutting aggressively.
'Don't play games, Safiyah. You know it is.'

'How could I?' She frowned up at him. 'You're saying
this…' she gestured to the article '…isn't a hoax?'

Karim surveyed his wife, his annoyance giving way to
dawning disbelief. Her skin had paled as if she'd received
a shock. That, surely, wasn't something she could feign.

Gently he took the tablet and put it down.

'Karim? What's going on? Why would anyone print
such a story?'

He watched the throb of Safiyah's pulse in her throat.
Surely only a consummate actress could pretend to be so
stunned? Yet this *couldn't* be a surprise to her.

'You know it's the truth. You heard it five years ago.'

'Five years ago?' She frowned.

'When you came to meet me in the palace courtyard
that night.'

The night he'd been torn between lust and the determination to do no more than kiss her lest he take advantage
of an innocent under his roof.

She blinked, her eyes round. 'I didn't go to the courtyard. That was the evening we heard Rana was sick. Father

and I packed up and went home that same night. He left a formal apology and I wrote you a note.'

Karim's lips curled. 'A note that said only that you were sorry you'd had to leave so quickly. That something urgent had come up.' A brush-off, in fact.

Safiyah shook her head like someone surfacing from deep water. 'I thought I'd have a chance to explain the details later, in person.'

When he didn't respond, she switched back to the news story. 'You're saying your father wasn't the Sheikh of Za'daq? *Really?*'

Karim stared into those velvet-brown eyes he knew so well and felt the earth tilt off its axis.

She hadn't known. She really hadn't known.

All this time he'd believed Safiyah had snubbed him when she'd discovered the truth of his birth. For one golden illuminated second joy rose. She hadn't spurned him after all.

But she would now. Nothing surer. She'd be horrified at the scandal. And then there was the way he'd treated her. Believing she'd dumped him, he'd refused to take her calls, deleted her messages. And, more recently, he'd forced her into marriage.

Karim reeled as the truth sank in.

He'd thought she'd understood who she was marrying.

This news threatened both his crown and the relationship he and Safiyah were building. It could yank both from his grasp.

He looked at his wife and a wave of regret crashed through him.

Suddenly Karim knew fear. Bonedeep fear.

CHAPTER ELEVEN

'WHO WAS YOUR FATHER, then?' Safiyah could barely take it in.

Karim shrugged wide shoulders. 'I don't know.'

'Don't *know*?'

Karim wasn't a man to live with doubt.

'Presumably the man my mother ran off with.' His voice was bitter. 'Though that's pure assumption. Maybe she had several lovers.'

'You didn't ask her?' It didn't seem possible that he hadn't pressed to find out.

'She died of pneumonia when I was a child. There was no one else to ask.'

Except her lover—the man who might be his father.

What must it be like, not knowing who your parent was?

She frowned. It would be worse for Karim, since his mother hadn't been around for much of his childhood. The only parent he'd had was the irascible old Sheikh—a man she'd found daunting and her father had described as arrogant with a mean streak.

'I'm sorry, Karim.'

Another tiny lift of the shoulders but his expression didn't lighten. Instead his gaze drilled into her.

'Surely the rest isn't true? You and your brother seem to be good friends. He didn't really banish you?'

Karim snorted. 'That's nonsense. I decided to step

aside from the crown. I actually had to persuade Ashraf to take it.'

'So,' she said slowly, 'it was your decision to leave Za'daq?'

He nodded. 'The last thing my brother needs is me hanging around. He's a good man—a fine leader. But there are conservative elements in Za'daq who'd prefer me to be on the throne because I'm the elder.' He laughed, but the sound was devoid of amusement. 'Though they won't feel that way now the truth is out.'

Safiyah disagreed. From what she could tell, most of the support for Karim had been because, while supporting his father, he'd proved himself an able statesman, fair and honest. He'd worked hard and achieved respect. The truth of his birth would be a shock, but it didn't change his record.

Safiyah wrapped her arms around her middle, torn between sympathy for Karim and hurt that he hadn't trusted her enough to tell her this before. But why would he? They didn't have that kind of relationship. Their closeness was only in bed.

She looked up to find his gaze fixed on her so intently she almost felt it scrape past her flesh to her innermost self. She looked away. That was nonsense—a product of sexual intimacy. But more and more she found herself stunned by how *close* she felt to Karim. As if with a little effort all those romantic dreams she'd once held could come true.

Except when reality intervened, reminding her they didn't have that sort of relationship.

'You thought I knew all this?'

Karim's expression was hard to read, yet she could have sworn he looked uncomfortable.

'That evening we were supposed to meet...'

He paused, giving her time to recall her excitement and trepidation at the plan to meet him alone. She'd been so in love, so sure of his affection—though he'd never come right out and said the words—that she'd been persuaded to break every rule.

She'd thought the night would end in his bed. Instead it had ended with her romantic daydreams smashed.

'Yes?'

'I was waiting for you when Ashraf arrived instead. He had the results of some medical tests. We'd been looking for bone marrow donors to extend the Sheikh's life.' Karim's mouth twisted. 'The old man had always believed Ashraf wasn't his son, but Ashraf was tested anyway—out of sheer bravado, I think. One test led to another and the results proved just the opposite. I was the illegitimate one—not Ashraf.'

Safiyah wondered how she'd been so blithely unaware of the undercurrents at the Za'daqi court. But then she'd been lost in the romance of first love—only love.

'I still don't see how—'

'Later I discovered you and your father had disappeared in the night with an excuse about a family problem. I assumed you'd overheard our conversation since it took place where we were supposed to meet.' His chin lifted as if challenging her to deny it.

Reading the pride in that harshly beautiful face, Safiyah guessed what a blow the news of his birth had been to a man raised as a royal, with every expectation of inheriting a throne. She breathed deep, imagining what it was like to have your world turned on its head.

She didn't have to imagine too hard. She'd had her life snatched off course not once but twice, her own hopes and goals destroyed when she'd been forced into marriages she didn't want.

'I see,' she said, when she finally found her voice. 'You thought I hid in the shadows and eavesdropped.' Safiyah felt something heavy in her chest—pressure building behind her ribs and rising up towards her throat. 'Then persuaded my father to make up some excuse to leave? As if he wasn't a man who prided himself on his honesty?'

She'd hated the subsequent marriage her father had pushed her into but he'd done it for what he'd believed to be good reasons. He'd been a proud, decent man.

'As if *I*...'

The stifling sensation intensified, threatening to choke her breathing. She forced herself to continue, her chin hiking higher so she could fix Karim with a laser stare.

'You thought I abandoned you when I discovered you weren't going to be Sheikh. That all I cared about was marrying a king? That I didn't have the decency to meet you and tell you to your face?'

Safiyah choked on a tangle of emotions. Disappointment, pain, distress. How could he have believed it of her? He knew nothing about her at all! She'd been in love, willing to risk everything for a night alone with him, and he'd believed *that* of her.

She swung away, fighting for breath. Through a haze she saw Tarek, running in circles, trailing his precious kite.

'You have to admit the timing fitted,' said Karim.

Yes, the timing fitted. Drearily, Safiyah thought of how fate had yanked happiness away from her. But Karim hadn't loved her. If he had, he'd have at least stopped to question his awful assumptions.

She turned to him, seeing not the man she'd once adored, nor the passionate lover who'd introduced her to a world of pleasure. Instead she viewed the man who'd thought the worst of her—and her family. Who'd refused to give them the benefit of the doubt, treated them with contempt.

No wonder he hadn't returned any of the increasingly desperate messages she'd left all those years ago. He'd excised her from his life with ruthless precision.

The choking sensation evaporated and Safiyah dragged in lungsful of clean sea air. They felt like the first full

breaths she'd taken in years. For too long she'd lived with
regret over the past. She'd hidden it away, pretended the
pain wasn't there while she tried to make the best of life.
Now, like glass shattering, regret fell away. With clear eyes
she faced the man who'd overshadowed her emotions for
too long.

'Yes, it was a coincidence. But, believe it or not, the
world doesn't revolve solely around you and the Za'daqi
royal family.'

'Safiyah, I—'

She raised her hand and, remarkably, he stopped. It was
as if he sensed the change in her. The tide not of regret and
hurt, but of cold, cleansing disdain. For the first time she
could remember Safiyah looked at Karim and felt no yearning, felt nothing except profound disappointment.

'The night you heard you were illegitimate my father and
I discovered Rana needed us.' A quiver of ancient emotion
coursed through her, that dreadful fear that had stalked her
too long. 'She'd tried to kill herself.'

'Safiyah!'

Karim stepped closer, as if to put his arms around her,
but she moved back and he halted. Deep grooves brack-
eted his mouth and furrowed his brow and Safiyah read
genuine concern.

'I had no idea.'

'No—because you never gave me a chance to explain.'

He recoiled as if slapped, his face leached of colour.
Strange that Safiyah felt no satisfaction.

'Tell me?' he said eventually.

'Rana was living in the city, studying to become a vet.
But university life didn't suit her, and she found the city
challenging after being brought up in the country. Plus, although we didn't know at the time, she was being stalked
by another student. There had been harassment and she
felt isolated, afraid to go out. She became anxious and de-

pressed. I knew something wasn't right, but on the phone she sounded…' Safiyah swallowed. 'She overdosed on tablets.'

'I'm sorry, Safiyah. Truly sorry.'

Karim's face was sombre, and she knew he wasn't just referring to her sister, but to all his assumptions about Safiyah's character and actions.

It was easier to focus on Rana. She didn't want to talk about herself. 'I think the shock hastened my father's death. He went downhill fast after that.'

The speed of his illness and his desperation to see at least one of his daughters settled had broken down her resistance to marrying Abbas.

'My husband arranged for Rana to have excellent support. She's doing well now. She enjoys working on a horse stud and she's even talking about doing part-time study.'

Karim was reeling. His feet were planted on the ground but he felt as stable as Tarek's kite, swooping too low towards a bush. All this time…

What must it have been like for Safiyah, watching her father die, worrying about her sister and facing the blank wall he'd erected to prevent any contact between them?

He swallowed hard and it felt as if rusty nails lined his throat. He'd failed her when she'd most needed him.

He winced, remembering how she'd said her husband had arranged support for Rana. Her husband Abbas. Karim had felt jealous of Abbas, and at the same time triumphant that Safiyah's passionate nature hadn't been awoken till he, Karim, married her. But there was more to being a husband than orgasms. Whatever his faults, Abbas had been there for her. She still thought of him as her husband.

How did she think of him?

As the man who'd shunned her? The man who'd blackmailed her into a marriage she didn't want?

He could argue that he was protecting her son, but should her body and her life be forfeit because of that?

Karim considered himself honourable.

Today he realised how far short he fell of that ideal.

'What now?'

Karim dragged his gaze back to Safiyah. Suddenly she looked so small. Minutes ago, as she'd sparked with indignation, she hadn't seemed so diminutive. Now her arms were wrapped tight around her slender body as if she were holding out the world. Or holding in hurt.

Guilt scored pain through his belly.

Most of the time her presence, her vitality, made Safiyah seem larger than life. Now he saw her vulnerability, her hurt. He wanted to protect her, to haul her close and repeat his apology till she forgave him and looked at him again with stars in her eyes.

Fat chance of that.

She hated him.

He'd abused her trust and, because he'd grown up in a world where distrust and double-dealing were the norm, he'd believed the worst of her.

Yet, despite his mistakes, the idea of letting her go was impossible.

'Karim? What are you going to do now the story is out?'

He raised his eyebrows. Did she think he might cower here?

'Go back to the capital. Consult with the Council. Write a press release, then get on with the job of ruling.'

Except it might not be his job for long. Now that he was Sheikh the Council couldn't oust him. Yet Karim didn't want to rule a country that didn't want him. That bitter truth, like the knowledge of how he'd failed Safiyah in the past, curdled his gut. He'd offer the Council his abdication if that were the case.

When he'd been offered the role of Sheikh he'd been

assured it was because of his character and his record as a statesman, not his supposedly royal lineage. What if it wasn't true? What if the stain of his birth was too much for his new country to stomach?

Karim inhaled slowly, deliberately filling his lungs. He'd suffered the fallout of his illegitimacy once, with devastating effect. If he had to do it again, no matter. He had a full and interesting life to return to.

Except that was a lie. Even after a mere couple of weeks Karim knew that *this* was the life he craved. He thrived on the challenges and rewards of his new role. Including his newfound family. Would Safiyah stick with him if he left Assara? Could he ask it of her?

'You're not concerned about a swing of support away from you?'

Had she read his mind?

'To Shakroun, you mean?'

Karim guessed Shakroun was behind this press story. His rival hadn't had the numbers to mount a public challenge, but trying to tarnish Karim's reputation by backhand methods seemed like the man's style.

'Don't worry, Safiyah, whatever happens I'll protect you and Tarek from him.' Shakroun would get his hands on them only over Karim's dead body.

Safiyah surveyed him sombrely, her expression drawn and her eyes dark with shadows.

Reading that look, Karim felt a fist lodge in his ribs and his lungs heaved. 'What do *you* think about it?'

'I think you need to see the Council as soon as possible. Lobby key people and sound them out—'

'I meant what do you think about my birth? About the fact I wasn't really a prince of Za'daq?'

She'd thought him an aristocrat. In reality he was nothing of the sort. Karim swallowed and pain ground through him. His station in life would have an obvious impact on his wife. Pity he hadn't thought of that before.

Safiyah's features drew in on themselves. Her eyes narrowed, her skin tightened across her cheekbones and her generous mouth tucked in at the corners. Her nostrils flared in an expression of disdain.

'You do it so well, Karim. I have to wonder if it's a natural talent or whether you have to work at it.'

'At what?' Karim drew himself up, ready to fight however he must to hold on to what was his.

'At insulting me.'

The words smashed against him, making him blink.

'You didn't have a high opinion of me all those years ago and it seems nothing has changed.'

Safiyah pushed her shoulders back and lifted her chin, and abruptly she seemed to grow in stature. Less crumpled and disillusioned lover and more imperious queen. Despite the fire flashing in her glare, Karim felt relief eddy deep inside him. He preferred her fiery to defeated and hurt.

'It was a simple question. I have a right to know what you think.'

Her fine eyebrows arched. 'Do you, indeed? When the only reason I know the truth is because someone else broke the story? When *you* didn't trust me with it!' She prodded his chest with her hand then quickly withdrew, as if she couldn't even bear to touch him.

'I apologise. I thought you already knew.'

Safiyah sighed. 'What I think doesn't matter, does it? We're stuck with each other.' She lifted her hand to her forehead as if trying to rub away an ache.

'Safiyah…' He stepped closer. He had to know.

For years he hadn't cared what others might think if they knew the truth of his birth. But he cared what Safiyah thought. More than he'd believed possible.

Her hand dropped and her eyes flashed. 'Yes, it's a surprise, but I don't care if your father was a sheikh or a vagrant. What I care about is whether I can trust the man I married. Right now I have my doubts.'

She spun away and gathered up Tarek. Her actions were decisive and distancing. They made Karim feel the way he had as a kid, when he'd tried and failed to please the Sheikh, who had expected nothing short of perfection.

Karim set his jaw. He mightn't be perfect. He might be as flawed as the next man. But he'd be damned if he'd allow anyone to wrench away what was his.

And that included his wife and child.

CHAPTER TWELVE

'IT'S ALMOST TIME, Your Majesty. Just a few minutes.' The technician nodded encouragingly, as if Karim were a stranger to microphones and cameras.

Karim glanced at the notes before him on the vast desk and pushed them aside, ignoring a stifled protest from one of his secretaries. He preferred to speak direct to the camera since the broadcast would be live to the people of Assara. He had no need of prompts.

What he needed, or at least wanted, was to know where Safiyah was. Since they'd returned to the capital he'd barely seen her. Every time he went to talk to her she was missing. 'Out', the staff said.

Because she couldn't bear to be with him?

The idea fed the hollow sensation inside him. His wife found him wanting not due to his birth, but because of the way he'd treated her.

To a man who prided himself on doing the right thing, the knowledge ate like acid, eviscerating him.

The door opened to whispered urgent voices. Then he caught a flash of red and a high, childish voice. He pushed back his chair and stood. 'Let them in.' It was Safiyah— and Tarek too.

Karim's heart hammered his ribs, climbing to his throat as he took her in. She sailed towards him, ignoring the minders who would have kept her out. She looked magnificent and beautiful in a dress of glowing crimson. Her hair was piled high and she wore no jewellery apart from her ruby and diamond wedding ring and matching earrings that swayed against her neck as she walked, emphasising the purity of her slender throat.

Their gazes meshed. She was here for him. To offer her support despite the chasm between them.

Karim's chest tightened, filled with a swelling bundle of sensations. He swallowed roughly.

His wife. His Queen.

She was regal, and stunning—and, he realised, the only woman ever to have power over him.

Just watching her approach battered him with competing emotions. Desire, pride and fear that he'd irrevocably destroyed any softer feelings she might once have harboured. For those eyes locked on him were coolly guarded, giving nothing away.

He'd given up pretending that it didn't matter. The news that he'd been wrong about her all this time had stripped all pretence away. He wanted his wife in every way. Not just her sexy body but her admiration, her kindness and her gentle humour.

Beside her marched Tarek, wearing fine clothes and a slight frown, as if he were concentrating hard. Karim felt a pang at the sight of him, remembering how it had felt as a young child, trying to be the perfect little Prince everyone expected.

'Safiyah.'

Karim started forward. But instead of taking his outstretched hand she sank into a curtsey, clearly for the benefit of their audience. Beside her Tarek bowed—a deep, formal, courtly bow.

Karim saw the Councillors on the other side of the room note the gestures of respect and nod to each other, as if approving this confirmation of the Sheikha's loyalty.

When she straightened Karim took her hand and pulled her to him, Tarek too. 'Where have you been?' His tone was sharper than he'd intended, but he'd felt stymied, not being able to find her.

Safiyah's eyes flashed, but she said evenly, 'In the city.' As if that explained everything.

The technician approached, hovering uncertainly. Safiyah nodded to the man and smiled, then turned to Karim. Her voice was low, for his ears alone. 'I thought it might help if we were beside you, Tarek and me, when you do your broadcast.'

'As a show of solidarity?' Karim felt his eyebrows rise. It wasn't a bad idea, politically speaking. Beyond her he saw senior government ministers, nodding in approval at the family group they made.

Before she could answer he shook his head. 'I appreciate your support, Safiyah, and yours too, Tarek.' He smiled at the boy, who was looking far too solemn, and ruffled his hair. The kid relaxed a little then and smiled back, leaning towards his mother. 'But this is something I need to do alone. I won't have anyone accuse me of hiding behind my wife's skirts, beautiful as they are.'

Safiyah stared up into stunning eyes and felt a flurry of emotion ripple through her. She saw pride there, and determination.

He took her hand, raised it slowly and kissed it.

Safiyah's knees almost buckled.

This was the man she'd fallen in love with all those years ago. The man she'd given her heart to. Who, if he only knew, still held that floundering organ in his keeping.

Fear settled in her bones. For though he smiled there was no softness in his expression. He was focused beyond her, on the challenge ahead. On the sheikhdom.

That was what mattered to Karim.

She, as a convenient wife, came a poor second.

Nothing had changed.

Except she'd discovered, faced with this crisis, that she *did* care for him. Had never given up caring. It was a burden she must learn to bear. A secret she'd have to live with.

She moved closer, leaning up to whisper in his ear. 'You haven't changed your mind, have you? You're not going to abdicate?'

'No.' He paused, then added, 'I want this too much to throw in the towel. But, no matter what happens, believe that I'll keep you and Tarek safe.'

She believed him. He would keep his word.

Karim looked past her, then to the technician. 'You and Tarek had better take a seat over there.' He gestured to some chairs clustered on the far side of the room.

And so it came to be that Safiyah was there for Karim's momentous broadcast. She ignored the questioning glances of politicians unused to having a woman present when government matters were being discussed. She hung on every word, and as she did so her respect for Karim grew.

His readiness to misjudge her in the past still rankled, but with time to cool down she'd acknowledged that the stress he had been under must have contributed to his actions.

Now, hearing him talk with simple honesty about his birth and his vision for Assara, Safiyah felt again a once familiar respect and pride.

He acknowledged the truth of the story about his heritage, and said that he'd told the Royal Council he would abdicate if the circumstances of his birth were considered an insurmountable problem. He also took time to sketch his plans for the nation if he were to stay as Sheikh, and ended by promising a final announcement in the near future.

When the broadcast ended Karim looked around the silent room at the powerful men, regarding him solemnly.

It was clear they hadn't yet made a decision on whether to support their new Sheikh. Thinking of the alternative, of Shakroun taking the throne, Safiyah shivered. How could they even consider letting that man into the palace?

Holding Tarek's hand, she made for the door, leaving Karim to deal with the politicians. She had her own priorities. Women might not have an overt role in Assaran politics, but that didn't mean they didn't have their own networks, or that they didn't have any influence at all. Safiyah had already been busy accessing those networks on Karim's behalf.

He was the best man for the position. More, he was the man she loved.

She would stand by him no matter what.

In the days after the public broadcast Karim followed his schedule of regional visits just as if there wasn't an axe poised to fall on his neck if the Council decided his illegitimacy overrode his merits.

Another man—Shakroun, for instance—would have clung to his position, since constitutionally the Sheikh, once crowned, had absolute power. Karim wasn't that sort of man. Call it humility, or perhaps excessive pride, but he needed his new country to *want* him.

Meanwhile he got on with the job he was there to do. Listening to the people, solving problems and planning new directions. And at his side, day and evening, was Safiyah.

She was a revelation. He'd seen her performing her part at the wedding celebrations, and the way she'd stood up for him on the day of his broadcast had filled him with pride and gratitude. But his wife was far more than a beautiful face to adorn a royal event.

Safiyah charmed both the public and VIPs alike, her manner almost unobtrusive but incredibly effective at helping people relax in the royal presence. Time and again

Karim found her leading people forward so their concerns could be heard or their achievements noted. Nor did he miss the way she drew apart from the official entourage on site visits to listen to knots of women who gathered on the fringes of the VIP parties.

Had she supported Abbas in this way?

Karim's mind slewed away from the thought. She was *his* now, through thick and thin. He had no intention of letting her go.

Since returning to the palace he'd slept alone—partly because of the crazy hours he worked, but mainly because of the hurt in her eyes when she'd discovered how he'd mistrusted her. The bitterness in her voice as she'd recommended they keep their distance.

Tonight, surely, they could put all that behind them.

He grinned and knocked on her door, anticipation humming in his veins.

'Karim!' Her velvet eyes widened in surprise and he vowed that tonight he'd smash through the barriers that separated them.

'Aren't you going to let me in?'

She clutched her pale blue robe closed with one hand as she pulled the door wider. He stepped in and watched as she took her time closing the door. Her robe was plain, but on her it looked incredible. Karim devoured the sight of those bounteous curves, the spill of lustrous dark hair. Arousal stirred, thickening his veins and drawing his body tight.

She turned towards him, automatically raising her chin.

Safiyah might be soft and feminine but she was no pushover. He liked that, he realised.

'You've had news? From the Council?'

'Just now. The vote was unanimous. They want me to stay.'

For a second she shut her eyes and he saw a shudder run

through her. It was a reminder that it wasn't just Karim whose future had hung in the balance. Safiyah's had—and Tarek's.

'It's all over now,' he reassured her. 'I'll make a public announcement in the morning.'

She nodded and he watched her swallow convulsively. She'd hidden her fear well but clearly she'd been worried.

Karim smiled. 'I have to thank you, Safiyah. Not every woman would have stood by me the way you have. And you've done more than that. I appreciate the way you've worked to help me, both in public and behind the scenes.'

Her eyebrows lifted. Had she thought he hadn't been aware of her networking on his behalf? His staff had informed him of much he hadn't seen personally. It was one of the reasons he knew he could bridge the gap between himself and his wife.

He moved closer, but then she spoke. 'What choice did I have? You're my husband. My son's fate rests with you.'

It wasn't the words alone that stopped him. It was her tone—flat and bitter. As if she regretted being married to him. As if she had no personal interest in his fate.

For a second, and he didn't know why, he thought of his mother. Had she been bitter about marrying the man her family had approved for her? Had she wished from the beginning that she could escape?

But Safiyah wasn't like his mother, running away and leaving her children. Safiyah had done everything she could for Tarek—even accepting a marriage she didn't want.

Karim's pulse dipped at the thought. Things would be better between them now. He'd make sure of it.

He watched her wrap her arms around her slender waist, her mouth a flat line. Her body sent an unmistakable message of rejection, but he persisted.

'I know I hurt you, Safiyah, and I'm sorry for it. But I also know there was more to your actions than necessity.'

There had to be. Once he'd taken for granted that she cared for him. Lately, learning that she'd never betrayed him as he'd believed, Karim had found himself yearning again for that devotion. Strange to realise how empty his world had felt without it. He'd told himself during those years in exile that he'd been like a rudderless ship, because he'd been cut off from the life he knew. Now he realised it was this woman he'd missed—Safiyah he'd wanted as his anchor.

Her arms tightened, pulling the fabric over luscious breasts. Karim felt a kick of masculine response in his belly.

'What more could there be?' Her eyes were dull with denial.

Karim rocked back on his feet. He'd thought it would be simple. He'd apologised for hurting her and now, with this news, they could start afresh.

But Safiyah wasn't ready to move on. His chest clogged. Pain circled his ribs. She hadn't forgiven him. The tenderness she'd once felt had drained away. She had just helped him because they were legally tied.

He felt a fool. He'd imagined she'd worked tirelessly on his behalf, *their* behalf, because she cared about him—about them. Now it turned out there was nothing personal about what she'd done.

Hurt vied with anger. And with a dawning sense of loss so vast it threatened to engulf him.

'Safiyah. Don't talk like that. You know you want—'

'There's nothing I want, Karim. Not now I know your position is secure and Tarek is safe.' She hefted a deep breath. 'I'll see you in the morning.'

As if he were a servant to be dismissed!

Karim's jaw clenched, his body stiffening.

And yet Safiyah's body betrayed her. Karim saw her

nipples peak against tight fabric, the out-of-control flutter of her pulse.

A hint of musky feminine arousal tantalised his nostrils. His body quivered in response.

She might be trying to hurry him out through the door, but still she wanted him. He lifted his hand to stroke one finger down her cheek. Her eyelids fluttered, then she jerked her face away, staring back with dislike.

Yet she couldn't disguise the glow of amber heat in her eyes—a sure sign, he'd learned, of sexual arousal.

Heat punched his belly. Triumph surged. Safiyah might not want to want him, but in this at least they were still partners, each caught in the same tangle of desire.

'Don't lie, *wife*. You want me.' A heartbeat pounded through him, a second, a third. Her expression gave the confirmation he needed. 'And I'll happily take what's on offer.'

Even if his soul craved far more.

He wrapped his fingers around the back of her skull and stepped in close, lowering his mouth to hers with a slow deliberation that, since it gave her time to pull away, proved his point.

She was his, and she wanted to be his, at least in this.

Wife, he'd snarled at her, reminding her that she was his possession. His words held no tenderness and anguish arced through her from where his fingers cradled her head down to the very soles of her feet.

She longed for so much more—which was why she'd cut him off abruptly when he'd pressed her, almost as if he knew her secret weakness.

When he'd *thanked* her for her help everything inside her had rebelled. She didn't want Karim's gratitude. She wanted so much more. She craved his love.

Which illustrated how mismatched they were. She

couldn't afford to let him know how she felt. He already had too much power in this relationship. She had to stand strong against him.

Except when his lips met hers shock jolted through her. His mouth wasn't harshly impatient. It coaxed gently…a slow brush that tempted then moved on to her cheek, her throat, then back to linger and tease. Strong teeth nipped at her lower lip and fire shafted to her nipples then drove low into her body. Her knees trembled and she found herself grasping his upper arms.

With a muffled sound of approval he wrapped those strong arms around her, enfolding her in searing heat. Hard muscle bound her, and despite her intention to resist Safiyah melted closer.

A sob rose in her throat that she should be so weak. But the pleasure Karim offered was too much, even though she knew it was purely physical. This sense of rare connection was illusory, the product of wishful thinking.

He deepened the kiss, drawing her up against him and delving into her mouth as if he couldn't get enough of the taste of her. As if his need matched hers.

This didn't feel heartless. It felt like everything she craved. And, with a sigh that shuddered right to her heart, Safiyah gave herself up to him.

When he swept her high in his arms she didn't protest. Instead she leaned against his chest, her hand pressed to the place where his heart pounded like a jackhammer.

When he laid her on the bed and stripped her, his eyes glittering like priceless gems from the royal treasury, Safiyah arched her body to help him peel off her clothes.

When he came to her, naked, proud and virile, she closed her eyes rather than search for tenderness in his gaze. She could pretend for this short time that the brush of his hands across her bare flesh was loving.

And when finally Karim stroked into her, deep and

strong, and she shattered convulsively, she steadfastly refused to think or yearn or hope. She took the pleasure he gave and told herself it was enough.

It had to be. For it was all he could give.

CHAPTER THIRTEEN

SAFIYAH OPENED THE window and leaned out, inhaling the fresh morning air, trying to dispel her anxiety.

She reminded herself of how much she had to be thankful for.

Tarek was safe. Not only that, but after only a few months living with Karim he was thriving. The nervous little boy who had expected only brusque orders from Abbas was learning to relax under his adoptive father's encouragement.

Rana was well and happy, actually excited at the prospect of studying again.

Meanwhile, Hassan Shakroun, the man she'd so feared, was on trial with a number of his associates for kidnap, bribing officials and conspiring to murder. Safiyah shuddered.

It truly had been a lucky day when Karim had agreed to take the sheikhdom. Everything was working out so well.

And yet…

Her heart beat high in her throat as she turned to look at the pregnancy test on the bathroom's marble counter. She didn't want to see the result.

The chances of a baby were slim. She'd begun taking contraception as soon as she'd realised theirs wasn't going to be a paper marriage. Yet since then Safiyah hadn't had a normal period. She'd ascribed that to stress, upsetting her cycle. Until yesterday, when she'd folded her arms and noticed her breasts were tender.

Safiyah bit her lip and breathed deep, chastising herself for her fear. Forcing herself closer, she picked up the stick and read the result.

Pregnant.

The indicator blurred before her eyes as her hand shook.

She was having Karim's child.

Safiyah groped for the counter-top, grabbed it as she swayed.

She shook her head. Why was she shocked? Hadn't she known in her heart of hearts that there was a child? There'd been mornings where she hadn't been able to face breakfast, and that underlying sense that something was different.

She opened her eyes and stared into the mirror, taking in the too pale features of the woman peering back.

The fact was she'd made herself pretend pregnancy wasn't possible even though she knew no contraceptive was foolproof. Even though she and Karim had a highly charged sex-life. He spent every night with her, and she couldn't remember a night when one or the other hadn't instituted sex.

Her mouth twisted grimly. At least she had the terminology right. It wasn't making love as far as Karim was concerned. It was just sex. Convenient, explosive and satisfying. And she was so weak, so needy when it came to Karim, that far from repulsing him she was greedy for his touch.

Her hand smoothed over her flat belly.

There was nothing convenient about this child. Yet, despite the circumstances, she wanted this baby. Warmth spread through her as she contemplated this new, precious life. She'd do everything in her power to protect and nurture it. No doubt Karim, too, already so good with his adopted son, would love his own child to bits.

Her fears weren't for the baby, who would grow up cared for by both parents. Her concern was for herself.

She sucked in a breath that was half a sob.

Bringing another child into this world, even knowing it would be loved and cared for, revealed the stark contrast with her own situation. Unloved. Unwanted except as a convenience. As a means of propping up Karim's claim to the throne and to breed him heirs.

Pain sheared through her as the ugly truth hit her full force.

She was pregnant *again* by a man who didn't love her. Who'd *never* love her.

Her place in his life was cemented fast—sex object, for as long as his passion lasted, royal hostess and brood mare.

And what would she do about it? What *could* she do? *Demand* he love her?

A bitter laugh escaped, scoring her throat as if with gravel shards. That would only reveal her feelings for him, when the one thing she had left was her pride. She intended to salvage that, at least.

There was no question of her deserting him. She had Tarek to consider, and this new child. She *had* to stay for their sakes.

She drew a slow, fortifying breath, feeling the accustomed weight of responsibility and duty cloak her shoulders. This time it seemed harder than ever to push those shoulders back and stand tall.

It didn't matter that she'd once had romantic dreams, or that she still yearned with all her secret inner self for Karim's love. She had his respect and his gratitude. For the moment she had his passion too.

Time to do what she'd had so much practice at doing—bundle up unwanted yearnings and bury them deep, in a dark recess where they'd no longer tease her.

'Safiyah?'

She spun round. Karim filled the doorway with his broad shoulders and loose-hipped stance. Instantly her insides plunged. The sight of him reinforced her fatal weakness.

Who was she kidding? It wasn't just duty that kept her in this marriage. She didn't have the strength to walk away from the man she loved.

'What is it?' He crossed the room in a couple of strides, grabbing her hands in his. 'You look pale as milk.'

'I'm fine.' Practice allowed her to stiffen her drooping spine. 'What are you doing here?'

He frowned down at her, clearly not convinced by her words. 'I knew you'd planned to ride this morning and I rearranged a meeting so I could ride with you. But you didn't show.'

Bittersweet regret filled her. She'd have enjoyed riding with him. Enjoyed even more the fact that he'd changed his diary to make time for her.

Because you'll take any crumbs you can get from him and be grateful, won't you?

The snarky inner voice hit low and hard, making her press a hand to her churning belly.

Karim looked down. 'What's that?'

Safiyah fought the impulse to whip her hand behind her back. She'd barely had time to take in the test result herself. But what was the point? Karim had to know at some point.

Silently she lifted her hand so he could read the result.

'Pregnant?'

His voice was stretched out of all recognition.

Pregnant!

Karim's head jerked back as emotion punched him. So much emotion. A jumble of feelings such as he'd never known. Pride. Excitement. Tenderness. Fear.

'You're having our child?' His voice wasn't his own.

He'd wondered about the possibility, then set the idea

aside. But now… Safiyah carried his flesh and blood inside her.

Karim dragged in a rough breath, trying and failing to fill his lungs. He didn't know how he felt about passing on genes from his unknown father to another generation. About creating a new life. Far better to concentrate on Safiyah.

'Are you sick?' His hold tightened on her wrists. She looked pale. No, not just pale. Drawn. 'Come on. You need to sit down and rest.'

His heart pounded at double speed as he watched her draw a slow breath. But instead of assenting she drew back, pulling out of his hold, putting her hands behind her as if afraid he'd touch her again.

Karim's stomach dropped. The way she stood there—shoulders back, eyes focussed on a point near his ear—returned him to the early days of their marriage. To a time when Safiyah had been unhappy.

Karim had begun to hope they'd got past that. She'd seemed more content, more at ease with him since the crisis when his illegitimacy had been broadcast. Increasingly he'd basked in Safiyah's gentle smiles, revelled in her ease with him—not just in bed, but at other times. He'd told himself the marriage was working.

He was taking things slowly, not pushing, content to let her set the pace, knowing that after his earlier mistakes he needed to move cautiously in building their relationship. Even if he chafed for more.

He didn't expect miracles, and knew he had a lot to make up for, but surely he hadn't been mistaken? He *knew* she enjoyed being with him. Surely her tenderness hadn't been a lie.

'Safiyah?'

The sound of her name seemed to jerk her out of her thoughts and she turned away, preceding him silently from the bathroom. She didn't stop in their bedroom but kept going to the sitting room, choosing an armchair rather than sitting on the comfortable sofa.

Karim told himself not to read too much into that, even though he wanted to hold her close. He poured a glass of sparkling water and handed it to her, noting that her fingers felt cool to the touch.

Shock?

'You don't seem happy about the news.'

Whereas he, after that initial blast of surprise, felt a glow of satisfaction he had to work hard to contain. Safiyah... pregnant with their child. His whole body seemed to throb with a new vibrancy at the prospect. Even those lingering doubts about his ability to be a decent father were scattered in the face of triumphant excitement.

He watched her swallow a sip of water and then turn to put the glass down, her movements slow and deliberate as if she feared she'd drop it.

He tried again. 'I know we didn't discuss another child, but—'

'It's all right, Karim.'

Her eyes lifted to his and he was stunned to read the blankness there. A terrible nothingness that settled like a shroud over his excitement, instantly suffocating his burgeoning joy.

'I know my duty. That's why you married me, after all. I knew you'd want a child. I just hadn't expected it so soon.'

'Safiyah...?' His flesh prickled at the eerie coolness of her voice. Where was the passionate woman he knew? The caring mother, the warm-hearted Queen, the seductive red-blooded wife? 'Do you mean you don't want our child?'

Karim heard the unsteadiness in his voice and didn't care. He felt as if an unseen fist had lodged in his gut. Hunkering before her, he took her hand.

She blinked and shook her head. 'Of course I want it.'

But she sounded choked, her voice husky as if she fought back tears. 'I just...'

Safiyah looked away.

Karim had had enough of barriers and distance. He lifted his other hand to her chin, turning her to face him.

'Tell me.' His voice was soft but commanding.

For a second her eyes glowed bright, then she looked down. 'I just need time, Karim. Bringing a child into a marriage like ours...' She shrugged and looked up again, her mouth twisting wryly. 'Ignore me. It's just pregnancy hormones.'

'No.' He leaned closer, into her space, sensing for the first time that they teetered on the brink of the indefinable problem that still lingered between them. 'What were you going to say?'

Safiyah's lips thinned as if she was holding back the words by physical force, but eventually they slipped out. 'It's what women do in arranged marriages—breed heirs. It's just that sometimes it feels...lacking.'

Lacking! Karim sank back on his heels, his heart racing and a dreadful queasy sensation rolling through his gut. His hand tightened on hers, as if to reinforce their connection. His other hand cupped her cheek, his thumb brushing across her mouth till it lost its prim flatness and softened against the pad of his finger. He felt the warm humidity of her breath against his flesh and awareness rippled all the way up his arm to his shoulders and neck.

Yet his stomach hollowed. He felt gutted, and a dreadful tight ache seared through his belly as her words penetrated.

He'd felt bereft the night he'd learned of his parentage. But this was worse. This was Safiyah—*his* Safiyah—saying that what they had wasn't enough.

The edges of his vision blackened. This time it was Safiyah who grabbed his hand, steadying him. So much for his careful plan to give her time to grow accustomed to them as a couple.

'Don't talk like that!'

'Why not? It's the truth.' She breathed deeply, as if marshalling her thoughts. 'You're a good man, Karim. A fine ruler. And you've been wonderful with Tarek. Better than I dared hope for. Don't worry. I'll accustom myself in time.'

Accustom herself! As if it were a state of affairs she couldn't avoid. A royal obligation.

Which it was.

Safiyah had married him for Tarek's sake and to save her nation. She'd married dutifully and at first that had suited Karim completely.

But not now.

Karim exploded to his feet on a surge of restive energy. He marched the length of the room, spun on his heel and marched back.

Initially he'd told himself that Safiyah deserved no better. Then, later, when he'd understood the truth about her, he'd believed that if he worked hard enough he could make her care for him again as she once had, despite his mistakes. Yet it was only now, as he looked into her wan face and set features, that the full realisation of her sacrifice slammed into him.

Karim couldn't bear that she saw what they had as a necessity rather than a gift. Not when to him it was so much more.

He skidded to his knees before her, gathering her hands and drawing them against his thudding heart. He couldn't simply ignore her words about an arranged marriage, let them hang as if they meant nothing. Even if the alternative meant risking everything.

It would be the biggest gamble of his life, but he refused to imagine failing. Besides, he'd only held back because he hadn't wanted to put pressure on her.

'Our marriage is much more than that, Safiyah.'

She nodded, firming her mouth. Yet still she didn't meet his gaze. 'Yes, it's for the best. For Tarek and—'

'Much as I care for Tarek,' he murmured, 'this isn't about him. Or even about the little one you're carrying now.'

Karim felt a fillip of excitement, just speaking of their unborn baby, yet he couldn't allow himself to be distracted.

'Yes, there's also Assara. You're doing a wonderful job—'

'Not Assara, either.'

At his words her head jerked up, wide eyes catching his. How often he'd watched those velvety eyes haze with delight as he took her to rapture. How often he'd watched them dance with pleasure as they rode, or when they played with Tarek.

Karim turned her hands, pressing her palms to his chest where his heart thundered, letting her feel how she affected him.

'I want this marriage, Safiyah. I want *you*. I always have. Even when I pretended I didn't.'

Now the moment of truth was here Karim found it easier than he'd believed possible. He'd been taught to avoid discussing emotions, as if the mere mention of them would weaken his masculinity. What a crock that was. He'd never felt stronger or more determined.

Clamping her palms with one hand, he lifted the other to her face, feeling the dewy softness of her delicate flesh. 'I love you, Safiyah. I love you with every fibre of my being, with every thought and every breath I take.'

He paused and hefted air into his overworked lungs, watching emotions flicker across her features.

'Don't! Please don't!'

Safiyah tried to free her hands but he held them fast. She looked up at him with over-bright eyes. 'I'd rather you were honest with me than have you say what you think I want to hear.'

Her mouth crumpled, and with it something inside Karim's chest. He couldn't bear to see her hurting so.

It took a moment only for him to slide his arms around her and lift her high against his chest as he rose to his feet. From this angle he could see the wild throb of her pulse in her throat and her convulsive swallow.

Because he'd hurt her. Not just today but over years.

'I *am* being honest, Safiyah. For the first time ever I'm sharing how I really feel.' He paused, willing her to believe him. 'I don't know if I can ever make up for the mess I've made of things. When I believed the worst of you. When I never even followed up to make sure you were okay all those years ago.'

He strode to the long sofa and sank there, cradling her on his lap. It felt right, holding her like this, soft and warm in his arms. He never wanted to let her go. Surely it was a good sign that she didn't struggle to get away?

'I was hurting so much, Safiyah, because I loved you even though I hadn't admitted it to myself. But that's no excuse. You needed me and I turned my back on you.'

His voice cracked as he thought of her, scared for her sister, grieving for her father, faced with the prospect of marrying a stranger.

Dark eyes locked on his as she tipped her head back, and for once Karim didn't try to mask his feelings as he'd been trained to. His love for her swelled and filled him till he thought he might burst.

'Karim…?'

Her eyes, pansy-dark yet flecked with amber, held his so intently he felt raw inside, with everything he felt, every secret, laid bare. It was like facing his conscience.

'It's true, my love.'

He lifted her palm and pressed his mouth to it, scattering fervent kisses there. But not for long. This had to be said.

He held her wondering eyes. 'I was a proud, arrogant prince, used to attracting women, used to people pandering to my whims. I saw that you cared for me and I took that as my due, never bothering to question my own feelings. If I had I'd have realised that what I felt for you was unique. I'd never cared for any other woman the way I cared for you, Safiyah. After you'd gone I felt like I'd been torn in two, but I blamed that on my changed circumstances.'

He shook his head, amazed at his obtuseness.

'I couldn't bear to think of you—especially when I heard you were to marry Abbas. Because it hurt too much. I pretended it was fury I felt, hurt pride that you'd duped me into believing you cared.'

'I *did* care, Karim.'

Her hand curled around his, the first tiny positive sign from her. It made his heart contract. She'd cared for him once. But now...?

'When you came to me in Switzerland I behaved like a spoiled brat, trying to hurt you.'

'You succeeded.' Her mouth twisted, but her voice was stronger and her eyes shone. Hope rose.

'I've been so blind, my love.' He shook his head. 'So slow to realise *you* were the reason I came to Assara. Not because I wanted the crown but because I wanted to be with you. Become your husband.'

His words ran out and Karim was left listening to the sound of his heart throbbing out a frenetic pulse, looking for some sign he wasn't alone in this.

'You came here because of *me*?'

He nodded. The words had poured out of him—a torrent smashed free from a dam wall. Now he was spent. The rest was up to her. Would she believe him?

'Because you loved me?'

'*Love.* I love you.'

As Karim watched, her eyes filled with tears that spilled down pale cheeks.

'Ah, *habibti.* Please don't. I can't bear to see you so sad.'

He wiped her tears with his thumb but they kept falling. The sight broke him. Was it possible he'd destroyed all the feelings she'd once had for him?

A soft hand cupped his jaw. 'Silly man. I'm crying because I'm happy.'

'Happy?' Karim stared into her lovely face and saw that crooked mouth curve up in a smile that made his heart lift.

'Yes, happy.' Her smile widened. 'You really do have a lot to learn about women.'

Karim didn't argue. He was the first to admit his previous experience had been limited to casual encounters. Nothing that compared to this.

'Tell me,' he demanded, capturing her hand and kissing it.

'That I'm happy?'

Mischief danced in Safiyah's eyes, and for the first time the band constricting Karim's chest eased. He grazed his teeth along the fleshy part of her palm and she jumped, then leaned closer.

Her expression grew serious. 'I loved you all those years ago, Karim, and I never stopped.'

She swallowed hard and he felt the shadow of her pain.

'And now?' He didn't deserve her love, but he needed it. He'd never needed anything more. 'I can live without a crown, Safiyah. Without courtiers and honours. But I can't live without you.'

'Hush.' Her fingers pressed his lips. 'You don't need to. We have each other now.' She leaned close, wrapping her arms around his neck. 'I love you. Always have and always will.'

Karim opened his mouth to reply. To say something

meaningful and memorable. But for the first time ever words failed him. He drew his beloved wife up into his arms and kissed her with a tender ardour that told her better than words how he felt.

He vowed he'd show her every day of their lives together exactly how much she meant to him.

EPILOGUE

SAFIYAH STEPPED INTO the room and pulled up abruptly, seeing Karim alone by the window. It had been a risk, arranging this meeting, but one she'd believed worth taking.

Karim was a changed man—happy and positive and oh-so-loving, unafraid to express his emotions. Especially since their daughter Amira's birth. He doted on their little girl, while his relationship with Tarek grew stronger by the day. And with Safiyah he was everything she'd ever longed for.

But she knew the past cast long shadows. She couldn't change Karim's loveless childhood, but she hoped at least to ease the pain of his not knowing his parents. Which was why she'd tracked down the man Karim's mother had run away to. The man who might be Karim's father.

Seeing her husband's preternatural stillness, the air of barely contained energy vibrating from those broad shoulders, she guessed the meeting hadn't gone well.

Her hopes nosedived.

'You're alone?'

He swung to face her and her heart rocked against her ribcage when she read his expression. In a rush she closed in on him, wrapping her arms tight around his powerful frame.

'I'm sorry, Karim. I thought—'

'I know what you thought, *habibti*.' His mouth crooked

up at one corner in a tight smile. 'That it was time I made peace with the man who might be my father. And you were right.'

He gathered her in, then turned to look out the window. There, just emerging from the palace, was a rangy figure, shoulders straight and gait familiar. He paused, as if sensing their regard, and looked over his shoulder. Karim inclined his head and the man reciprocated, then walked away.

'Yet he's leaving?'

Was it crazy to have hoped the two might begin to build a tenuous relationship?

'No, just stretching his legs. We both need a little time to process things. He's accepted my offer to stay in the palace for a visit. To meet the family.'

No mistaking the pride in Karim's voice.

'He has?' Safiyah stared up at her husband, stunned.

His half-smile broadened into a grin that made her heart flutter. 'What you mean is you're stunned I invited him to stay. But then he *is* my father.'

'Oh, I *knew* it! You have the same walk…and the angle of your jaw…' She paused, searching his face. 'And you're all right with that?'

Karim raked a hand through his hair. 'They didn't know about me.'

'Sorry?'

Safiyah looked up at him with those lustrous eyes and he pulled her even closer. It had been a morning of revelations and powerful emotion. He found he needed the concrete reality of his darling wife to anchor him.

'When my mother ran away with him she had no idea that I was his son. He swears that if they'd realised she'd never have left me with the Sheikh.'

Karim believed him. His father wasn't what he'd expected. A proud yet gentle man, he was a schoolteacher in a remote mountain valley, devoted to the children he looked on as his own, never knowing till recently he had a son.

'He and my mother were deeply in love, but her family ignored that and arranged her marriage with the Sheikh. A lowly trainee schoolteacher wasn't considered good enough for her. They were only together once before the wedding— one night of secret passion before a loveless marriage.'

Karim's thoughts strayed inevitably to Safiyah's dutiful marriage to Abbas. How desperate must she have felt, knowing there was no escape, giving herself as a convenient wife?

Safiyah had given him a whole new perspective on his mother. A new sympathy for a woman caught in an unwanted, unhappy marriage.

'When I was born my mother believed I was the Sheikh's son.' Karim drew a slow breath. 'According to my father...' He paused on the word, testing its newness but liking it. 'She finally left the Sheikh because her marriage broke down. Emotional abuse turned into physical abuse and she feared for her safety. But she always believed he wouldn't lay a hand on me or Ashraf as his precious heirs.'

'Oh, Karim...' Safiyah gripped him tight.

'My father didn't even know she'd run away from the palace till she came to him and they fled together over the border. They only had a year together before she died.'

'That's so sad.'

He looked down into her soft eyes. 'At least they had that.'

'You're turning into a romantic, Karim.'

He smiled, and looked at Safiyah as the shadows inside eased. 'How could I not be when I have you, *habibti*? It's all your influence.'

'And in all those years he never took another wife?'

Karim shook his head. 'Another thing my father and I have in common. It appears we're one-woman men.'

'Sweet talker.'

He pulled his beloved close and stroked his hands over the gossamer-fine silk of her dress. It shimmered, indigo blue, over her delectable curves. Inevitably he felt the familiar tug of desire and satisfaction. This woman was his life, his home—everything he wanted.

'Just stating the truth.' He moved his hands more purposefully and heard Safiyah's breath snare. Anticipation quickened his pulse. 'But they say actions speak louder than words. Perhaps I should demonstrate my feelings.'

He backed her towards the long divan by the window.

'We've got an official lunch in half an hour and—'

'Some things are more important than royal duty, my love.'

Safiyah shook her head, but she was laughing as he lowered her onto the cushions. 'You're right, Karim. Some things are.'

Then she reached for him, using those supple, clever hands so effectively that Karim forgot everything but the need to show his wife just how he felt about her.

* * * * *

COMING SOON!

We really hope you enjoyed reading this book. If you're looking for more romance, be sure to head to the shops when new books are available on

Thursday 17th October

To see which titles are coming soon, please visit **millsandboon.co.uk/nextmonth**

MILLS & BOON

Coming next month

BOUND BY THEIR NINE-MONTH SCANDAL
Dani Collins

"Señor Navarro," she said, offering her hand.

"Angelo," he corrected. His clasp sent electricity through to her nerve endings as he took the liberty of greeting her with, "Pia."

"Thank you for coming," she said, desperately pretending they were strangers when all she could think about was how his weight had pressed her into the cushions while her entire being had seemed to fly.

His eyes dazzled, yet pinned her in place. There was an air of aggression about him. Hostility even, in the way he had appeared like this, when she had literally been on the defensive. He seemed ready for a fight.

She had almost hoped he would leave her hanging after her note. She could have raised their baby with a clear conscience that she had tried to reach out while facing no interference from this unknown quantity.

As for what would happen if he did get in touch? She had tried to be realistic in her expectations, but Poppy had stuck a few delusions in her head. They seemed even more ridiculous as she faced such a daunting conversation with him. How had she even found the courage to say such frank things that night, let alone *do* the things they'd done? Wicked, intimate, carnal things that caused a blush to singe up from her throat into her cheeks.

"I need a moment," she said, voice straining.

She had already declined invitations for drinks, fearful her avoidance of a glass of champagne would make her condition obvious. She only had to say a last goodbye to the committee and, "Thank you again, but I must take this meeting."

Moments later, trembling inwardly, she led Angelo into the small office off the lab where she had worked the last three years when not in the field. She had already packed her things into a small cardboard box that sat on the chair. She was shifting from academic work to motherhood and marriage. That was all that was left of her former life.

Angelo seemed to eat up all the air as he closed the door behind him and looked at the empty bulletin board, the box of tissues and the well-used filing cabinet.

Pia started to move the box, but he said, "I'll stand."

He was taller than her, which made him well over six feet because she had the family's genetic disposition toward above average height. His air of watchfulness was intimidating, too, especially when he trained his laser-blue eyes on her again.

"Your card was very cryptic," he said.

She had spent a long time composing it, wondering why he had sneaked into the ball when he could easily have afforded the plate fee. At the time, she had thought his reason for being on the rooftop was exactly as he had explained it—curiosity. She had many more questions now, but didn't ask them yet. There was every chance she would never see him again after she told him why she had reached out.

Memories of their intimacy that night accosted her daily. It was top of mind now, which put her at a further disadvantage. Her only recourse was to do what she always did when she was uncomfortable—hide behind a curtain of reserve and speak her piece as matter-of-factly as possible.

"I'll come straight to the point." She hitched her hip on the edge of her desk and set her clammy palms together, affecting indifference while fighting to keep a quaver from her voice.

"I'm pregnant. It's yours."

Continue reading
BOUND BY THEIR NINE-MONTH SCANDAL
Dani Collins

Available next month
www.millsandboon.co.uk